MUROR – ATLANTIS
14,000 B.C. CHRONICLES

First Edition Design Publishing

Muror – Atlantis 14,000 B.C. Chronicles
Copyright ©2014 serrAA

ISBN 978-1506-912-47-9 PRINT
ISBN 978-1622-876-42-6 EBOOK

LCCN 2014941559

June 2014

Published and Distributed by
First Edition Design Publishing, Inc.
P.O. Box 20217, Sarasota, FL 34276-3217
www.firsteditiondesignpublishing.com

MUROR – ATLANTIS 14,000 B.C. CHRONICLES

By
serrAA

ATLANTIS 14000 BC

OUTPOST

SEMIRA

POSEIDIA

GADES

TULAN

IBERIA

THARSIS

LIXUS

CHAPTER 1

IT WAS 14,000 B.C.

In another time, in a place that no longer exists – Torr; a young Murovian priest, recently assigned to the Sailors' Temple in the city of Liss, was about to embark on a trip that would involve him in world historic events.

While Torr was packing what he needed for a trip to Nalta – the capital of the Murovian Empire – on the other side of the bay, on higher ground, a man stood by a window facing the city; it was Kalac, a High-Priest; he too was traveling to Nalta in the early morning. As Kalac looked at the city lights he pondered on the reason for the convening of the Head (Legislative Assembly). Meetings were never held during the week that the athletic games were scheduled.

Kalac was told that there was no need for him to get there so far ahead of the other members of the Head; they will need ten days to reach Nalta. Kalac could get there in less than half-an-hour if he were to use his airship, but, instead decided to travel by boat this time, a ten day trip.

It was long ago, Kalac couldn't remember the last time he saw the countryside at ground level; this seemed a good opportunity of doing so again. He must leave before dawn if he was to reach Nalta in the morning of the tenth day, so he called one of his servants and told him, "I'm taking the early boat to Nalta. Have a hound-cart (two-wheeled chariot) ready before dawn. You will drop me off at the river dock."

"It will be done, the hound-cart will be by the front door before dawn," the servant said.

******

In the morning, before dawn, a hound-cart was already waiting by the front door. As soon as Kalac came out of the house the two enormous black hounds hitched to the cart came alive; they were ready. Kalac dropped a bag into the cart and called his servant.

Soon they were on their way. Not long after they left the house the reflected splendor of the sun began to peep over the Eastern horizon and the whole bay and city of Liss could be seen to their right.

The road was built out of closely fitted stone blocks. There was a continuous clinking-rumbling noise as they rode over the joints. When they were about to intercept the main coastal road they slowed down and swerved left. Secondary roads and streets merging with the primary roads were offset to the left before the junction. This wiggle to the left was there to force you to slow down and as a reminder that you must yield at the intersection ahead. At the intersection they made a right turn and headed for the city of Liss.

Now, to their left, on an orchard, slaves wearing their distinctive scarlet tunics could be seen harvesting citrus trees. A work leader – wearing a brown tunic – supervised their work.

The color of the tunics implied the wearer line of work; they were of a single specific color.

The priests always dressed in white tunics; the merchants, and anyone having to do with the manual trades in gray. The rest of the people, and the work force during their leisure time, dressed in multicolored tunics.

Reaching the outskirts of the city they slowed down and merged with the city traffic.

Further down the road at the seaport; the docked ships; the jewels incrusted in their figureheads glittering in the sun as the lapping waves swayed them in their moorings. Their red tipped oars stored and aligned in the vertical position, and sails furled. Most of the ships were now being loaded; getting them ready to sail with their new cargoes around the continent or to a far off place across the seas.

Hound-carts, most of them six-hounded teams, went in and out of the port full of goods.

They stopped for a moment at an intersection to let a cart enter the port. Two men were talking by the roadside; one, a sea captain, the other, a brown-skinned man. The man was negotiating with the captain to become a slave worker in the captain's ship. Pre-paid workers commonly called slaves sold their services for a predetermined period of time.

At the Big River they made a left turn, heading south parallel to the river. On the other side of the river, to their right, on a hilly area, the big crystal tower – their powerhouse.

It was a huge crystal, about thirty feet high, enclosed within an insulating material and a metallic structure; the top faceted so that light rays from the sun, moon, or the stars would focus at certain points down the length of the crystal. From top to bottom faceted pyramidal surfaces were seen sticking out from the sides of the crystal; each one of them resonating at a different frequency. One frequency used to provide the illumination in public and private buildings, roadways, and waterways.

The torches used for illumination have tuned crystal circuits that generate the necessary electron flow to excite the conductive material found inside the tip of the torches.

During low light conditions or total darkness a sensor activated mechanism moves into position an electrode over the faceted top of the crystal to supply the needed light to keep the big crystal resonating. The electrode is energized by currents generated by applying intermittent stresses to other crystals; pre-wound counterweights are released to apply the pressure to their extreme ends.

There were eight powerhouses in the continent, one in each one of the eight principal cities. Their frequencies were relayed to the entire continent.

Continuing alongside the river they came across the market place. This early in the morning it was something to behold. The place resembled a beehive for the customers imitated the frantic dance of the bees as they darted from vendor to vendor. The vivid colors of their multicolored tunics produced a kaleidoscopic effect as their tunics fluttered in the wind.

Opposite the market square, at the river dock, the boat was being readied for the trip to Nalta.

Kalac dismissed his servant and went aboard.

The last of the cargo was now being stored away below the center walkway and between the oarsmen's benches. Soon they will be on their way.

Kalac's vision drifted in the direction of the boarding gate. A man wearing a white tunic was coming aboard. The young man was of the White race, a muscular hard bodied man with black hair and of above average height.

The white tunic meant that he was a priest, so Kalac went over to meet him. As Kalac approached the stranger he noticed that the young man radiated an aura of controlled power not commonly seen in such a young person.

"Welcome aboard! I am Kalac. Are you the new assistant priest assigned to the Sailors' Temple?"

"Yes I am, my name is Torr, and I'm on my way to Nalta to participate in the athletic games."

Kalac then told him, "After you store your bag come over and join me."

Torr headed for the sleeping area below the rear deck.

Topsides, a tent occupied the center of the rear deck; the quarters for the captain and important persons. The only beds in the boat were on this cabin-like tent. The rest of the passengers slept on hammocks below the rear deck. Kalac being a High-Priest was assigned the rear facing cabin; the forward facing one always the captains' quarters. There were benches for the passengers on both sides of this tent.

Great! – Kalac thought. It will be a productive trip; besides the original purpose he will have plenty of time to find out what college life was like these days – firsthand.

As Torr joined Kalac a man came around collecting the fare for the passage. The boat was ready to leave.

Oars were lowered and used to push the boat off the dock; then they took over. At the drummers' beat the big muscular Ayas oarsmen started their synchronized rowing; forty-eight of them, twelve pairs on each side.

Settling down to the drummers' cadence the boat seemed to become a possessed entity every time the red tipped oars propelled it forward.

Tall palm trees lined the river banks and the rising sun – to their left – would flash and sparkle on and off between the tops of the palm trees as the boat advanced.

Most of the oarsmen were from the Ayas Province, they were the best suited for such a demanding job. The Brown race was the tallest and strongest in the continent.

******

Five different races inhabit the planet; all originated in the continent of Muror. Genetic manipulation of the planet Homo sapiens by a race of dimensional travelers – the 'Seres' - created the actual intelligent races.

The White race – dominant in Muror – inhabits the Phara Province, the Brown and the Black races the Ayas Province, and the Yellow race the Oenic Province.

The fifth race, known as the Red race because of the color of their hair – reddish-blond – also originated in the continent of Muror; but, they were encouraged to migrate from the Motherland because of their attitude to life. They insisted in living for what they could get from others in order to satisfy their physical and materialistic desires; that made them incompatible with the values of the rest of the people of Muror.

They gradually migrated east, to an uninhabited land that existed between two continents and named it Atlantis, becoming a Murovian Colony.

As time went by they became a Murovian Kingdom; at that time the land was divided into ten provinces – each ruled by a Priest-King.

Many, many millenniums went by, then, a catastrophic event (28,000 B.C.) split the island continent into five islands. Most of the people survived the cataclysm but three of the Priest-Kings perished. The five remaining islands were then divided into seven kingdoms.

Eventually, Atlantis became an independent empire.

******

From now on, all the way to Nalta, every fifteen miles the oarsmen will be spelled at a relay station. Each stage takes about two and a half hours (a day was divided into twenty hours).

Passengers could come aboard or disembark at any of the relay stations.

Forty boats were always on their way to Nalta and forty heading back. Every five hours a boat would leave from Nalta and another one from Liss.

For the next ten days they will make their way south, half way down the continent of Muror, a distance of 1,200 miles.

SERES HOME PLANET —— ⬤
AL-EL HOME

CHAPTER 2

Meanwhile, at Semira; capital of the Atlantis Empire and of the island of Poseidia, Amelius – a royal scribe – was searching for some old records stored in the basement of the Royal Palace.

Finding the scrolls he was about to leave when a voice came out of one of the small ventilation holes.

"We must be careful."

It was the voice of Iltar the High-Priest. Some other voices assented to the statement but Amelius couldn't tell how many of them were there or who they were.

Iltar kept talking, "Meeting here is risky. In the future you will be contacted at your work place by somebody that I trust. He will be used as a go between. I can't be seen visiting military installations."

Somebody asked, "What about Muror? Will they intervene if they find out what we are up to?"

Iltar replied, "There is no reason for that to happen. The kingdoms that we will be dealing with are independent and they only have commercial ties with Muror."

What sounded like the previous inquirer stated, "We know that Muror doesn't have much of a ground army, mostly sailor-soldiers, but it is rumored that they possess weapons and technology far more advanced than ours."

"Yes general," Iltar said, "that is true. As you must be aware, from times immemorial there have been scattered reports from our vailxi (airships) pilots of encountering other ships – we must assume theirs – that could fly circles around ours when ours were flying at maximum speed, and faster than you could blink an eye they would disappear from view at fantastic speeds.

"You have visited Muror and observed their simple life style, that's how they want it. Hardly any of their secret scientific knowledge is applied in their daily life – but we know better. For 50,000 years Priest-Scientists have been trained to maintain and safeguard their secret technology and to pass it along to the next generation, all this in a secret location known only to a few of their leaders. It is true that Muror may have far more superior weapons, but, general, as I said before, what we are doing shouldn't concern them. There is nothing to worry about."

"I hope so," muttered the general; who then asked, "How about King Uranus?"

"Don't worry about him," Iltar answered. "He doesn't know what is going on. His mind is not what it used to be, I control him."

******

Uranus; King of Atlantis was the King of Kings. Besides being the King of Poseidia - one of the five Atlantis islands - Uranus also presided over the Council of Kings. The kings that ruled the other six kingdoms were free to do as they pleased in their kingdoms so long as their actions didn't conflict with the safety or interests of the Atlantis Empire.

The council presided by the King of Kings met whenever there was a conflict with the rules governing the empire.

******

A different voice was now heard asking, "What about the Queen of Mayax, has she consented to our demands?"

"Well...no, Queen Moo never accepted our terms," Iltar replied, "but everything came out according to plan. For reasons unknown, she left her brother Prince Coh in charge and went on a trip. Prince Coh is now the acting King of Mayax (Yucatan) and has accepted our terms.

From now on we'll start receiving a share of everything that we import from Mayax."

******

Most of the gold and silver used in Poseidia came from Mayax. In return Mayax received manufactured goods such as hunting weapons, tools, sandals, and clothing.

******

The general asked, "Have we started the contacts with the Uighur (China) and the Naga (India) Empires?"

"No, not yet," Iltar answered. "That's were your people come into play. An ambassador was all we needed at Mayax because a protection treaty already existed but the other kingdoms we have in mind are a different story, we only have commercial treaties with them and unlike Mayax they all have an army; a primitive one at that but still a concern since the use of force is not a desirable option. Our Air Assault Forces accompanying our ambassador will serve as a deterrent and at the same time showcase our military capabilities.

"Since there is not that much trade between our country and theirs; our share of the goods we buy from them, mostly spices and dyes, will not be enough. Instead we'll charge them a specific amount payable in precious metals."

A different voice was heard, "When do we start?"

Iltar answered, "First, I have to plan the mission and then convince Uranus to let us secure new military treaties; you will be contacted as soon as this is done.

"Please go now the same way you came in, one at a time, and make sure that you are not seen together when leaving the subterranean docks."

Amelius couldn't believe what he just heard; they were planning on using Poseidia's Military Protection Treaties to extort unauthorized payments for their own gain. Of one thing Amelius was sure – he recognized Iltar's voice. A general was also implicated in the plot but no names were mentioned and he didn't recognize any of the other voices.

It was evident that Uranus was not aware of what was happening. Was it safe to tell him? Amelius reasoned that there was a good chance that Uranus would not believe him. Due to his age and feeble condition Uranus trusted Iltar and the military leaders to carry on the affairs of state.

Amelius thought about contacting Chronus, Uranus' son; but he couldn't think of a safe way of doing so without raising suspicions.

Chronus had flown in his vailx to Sais in the Egyptian Delta to visit his daughter and to see for the first time his granddaughter – Misar. Thoth an Atlantis High-Priest and founder of Sais was the husband of Chronus' daughter.

Any messages transmitted to Chronus heir to the throne of Poseidia and of the Atlantis Empire would for certain be brought to the attention of the communication station master – a priest, who even if he wasn't implicated in the plot out of a sense of duty and suspecting a possible Uranus' health emergency would inform Iltar that Amelius, a royal scribe, was requesting from Chronus his immediate return to Semira.

Amelius decided that the safe thing to do was to wait for Chronus return.

******

Immediately after the meeting Iltar went to his office and tried to contact Esman; Poseidia's Chief Diplomat, but he was not in his office, so Iltar ordered his assistant to go and find him.

Esman and Iltar had been schoolmates, both studied for the priesthood but upon graduating from the Temple College Esman was not selected to be a priest, not everybody that graduated was. Eventually, Esman, with Iltar's help, became an ambassador.

It didn't take long, the assistant showed up with Esman and then returned to the adjacent office.

Before he sat down an anxious Esman asked, "How did it go? Did you reach an agreement?"

"Yes, we have the officers," Iltar replied; then added, "And of course the soldiers will do as they are ordered."

Esman asked, "Do the officers know about Chronus?"

"No, and they don't need to know. So far you are the only one that knows what our true intentions are. Chronus must die, in an accident, so that I can become the king and you the counselor to the king when Uranus dies. Hmm..., that ship of his."

They both laughed.

Iltar added, "Maybe, maybe after he gets back from his trip to Sais."

"Great idea" Esman said; then asked, "But how are we going to do it?"

"Leave it to me," Iltar said. "Chronus' vailx is kept and serviced at the air base. I'm sure that the general can do something about it."

"Yes...I see," Esman said.

"Well, I have things to do," Iltar said. "I'll keep you informed."

Then they parted company.

CHAPTER 3

It had been nine long days since they left Liss. As usual Kalac and Torr were up early.

When the sun broke over the horizon a continuously changing pattern of colors unfolded before their eyes as the sun's golden rays reached the multicolored cultivated fields that flowed around the low rolling hills.

The river banks were bursting with colors, flowers of many colors bloomed and lotus flowers floated by. The lotus flower was the heraldic symbol of Muror.

A local barge was leaving one of the tributaries that merged into the Big River and a few carts full of produce could be seen on the roads that bordered the river. There were roads on both riverbanks. Torches were located between the roads and the riverbanks, they served a dual purpose; at night, besides illuminating the road they guided the river boats.

A short time after, the boat made a right turn, left the river and entered the canal that will take them straight to Nalta – the last 125 miles. Now; on their right side the Phara Province and on their left side the Ayas Province.

******

Later that day while questioning Torr about his parents Kalac found out that Torr's Father was a healer and not a priest, and that the reason Torr was admitted to the Temple College was that he was born in one of the days dedicated to the Gods.

There were eighteen months of twenty days in Muror's solar calendar. The extra five days – between the nine and tenth month – dedicated to the Gods. Anybody born during those five days – if interested and chosen – was admitted to the Rowen Temple College on their twelfth birthday. The only other students admitted were the offspring of the priests or priestesses. After seven years of training only a selected few were chosen to the priesthood, the others joined Muror's workforce in different capacities.

******

All day and all night they traveled on the canal and about an hour before sunrise they reached Nalta.

On disembarking Torr headed for the stadium complex. As for Kalac, a cart from the temple was waiting for him.

The Great Temple wasn't that far from the docks so it didn't take long to reach it. The temple was an imposing stone building – it was huge; the exterior as simple and unadorned as their approach to life. The entrance guarded by two statues – a God and a Goddess; representing the Sun God and the Moon Goddess. Both statues adorned with silver and copper, embellished with precious stones.

The gatekeeper was expecting Kalac and ushered him to one of the dormitories reserved for such events. Kalac was then informed that the other members of the Head had arrived during the night and were now resting, and that the meeting was scheduled to be held at noon – right after lunch.

After escorting Kalac to his room the gatekeeper went over to inform the Archpriest that all the members of the Head were now present.

******

The Archpriest presided over the Head and was the maximum authority on religious matters, but it was the Headmasters who formulated the laws and ran the Murovian Empire with the Archpriest guidance and approval.

Besides the Archpriest and the Arch priestess the Head consisted of ten other members; Kalac, two High-Priests, two High-Priestesses, a General of the Army, a Harbormaster, and Representatives for the Farmers, Craftsmen and Merchants.

******

At the appointed time Kalac left his room and headed for the meeting room. All the members converged on about the same time. After the usual greetings they sat on stone blocks cushioned with animal furs. A larger stone in front of each seat served as a table.

A meal was served. During that time the talk was about the country state of affairs and the athletic games.

******

Right after the tables were cleared the Archpriest came into the room and said, "Good day people of Muror."

Everybody in the room stood up as a sign of respect. Once they sat down the Archpriest said, "The Arch Priestess is not present because she is taking care of important religious matters.

"Well, then, let's get down to business. One of our boat captains has brought us news about problems in the land of Mayax (Yucatan). It is true that we don't have control over our former colonial kingdoms but we must remember that we are the Motherland. We seeded the planet and it is our duty to watch over it.

"According to a Mayax palace source – a friend of one of our boat captains – whatever is going on happened when an ambassador from Poseidia-Atlantis visited Mayax.

"Our informant overheard Queen Moo angrily telling her brother Prince Coh that there was no way that she would go along with what the ambassador demanded. That's all the informant was able to hear, they stopped talking when he entered the room.

"Next day Queen Moo announced that for the time being her brother Prince Coh would be the acting ruler of Mayax. Next morning she sailed on a ship headed for the Inland Sea (Mediterranean Sea). We don't know her final destination; all we know is that the ship was scheduled to go as far as Sais the Atlantis Colony in the Lower (Egyptian) Delta.

"We have to send somebody to find out what is going on; whoever goes, among other things, has to be capable of flying an airship. The problem is that the Atlanteans know who our pilots are."

"Yes I see your point," the general said. "Eventually the investigation will take our man to Semira-Poseidia and they know Kalac and our two pilots. As for using other pilots; our Priest-Scientists, no way, their use is out of the question, we can't risk any of them; it takes years of training to become one. We need a new man for the job."

The Harbormaster interrupted and said, "What if our man is transported by one of our pilots to wherever he needs to go? When ready to return he can call the base and one of our pilots can pick him up."

"That may not be a good idea," the general said. "To return he will have to call the base and the signal could be intercepted."

"We agree with you general," articulated in unison the other members of the Head.

One of the priestesses added, "Remember, the person not only has to be capable of flying an airship but also must be fluent and familiar with the dialectal differences in our languages. In other words, we need somebody with a high scholastic level."

The Archpriest then asked, "Now...tell me; what are you people planning on doing?

After a moment of collective silence it was Kalac who said, "We must train the person. It will take about thirty days if the person is already trained up to a certain level, like a recently graduated priest; and I happen to know one."

"Who is this man?" inquired the Archpriest.

Kalac answered, "I met him on my way here. As far as I know he has never been in contact with any visitors from Atlantis or any other kingdom."

The Archpriest asked, "But, are you sure that he is up to the task?"

Kalac answered, "Yes, I'm sure of that. He is here in Nalta to participate in the athletic games."

The Archpriest asked, "Does the proposal have the Head approval?"

All the members of the Head assented to the proposal.

The Archpriest then said, "Well, if everybody agrees; so be it, you have my blessing. I leave it to Kalac to plan and implement the mission," he then stood up and said, "The Gods be with you," then left the room.

When the Archpriest left Kalac told the others, "I'll be in touch if I need your help. For the next thirty days or so I will be spending some of my time at our secret base. If for some reason you have to get in touch with me please transmit the message to my home, it will be relayed to me."

As soon as the members of the Assembly left the room Kalac went over to the gatekeeper and ordered that a cart be readied and brought to the front entrance. Then entering one of the small altar-rooms opened a concealed door and went down to a huge underground cavern where two airships were park; and ready to break their earthly bounds. He talked to one of the Archpriest pilots and told him to be ready to fly him and another passenger to Liss as soon as he returns from the Sports Stadium.

At the Great Temple entrance a hound-cart was waiting for Kalac; he rode it to the Sports Stadium Complex. There he left the cart in the parking lot, headed for the living quarters and went looking for Torr; found him in the company of other athletes and told him, "Let's take a walk, we need to talk."

Kalac's visit surprised Torr and made him wonder about the reason for his visit.

They left the building, sat on a park bench, and then Kalac gave an account of what was happening and his plan to train him. When asked if he would accept; Torr responded, "If you think that I can do it – I accept."

Kalac said, "I expected nothing less from you so I have already made arrangements. Let's get your things and be on our way, there is still much to be done today."

Back at the Great Temple they went to the underground cavern where the pilot was ready to go.

Torr couldn't believe what was happening to him. This morning he was getting ready to compete in the games. Now, he was about to climb aboard an airship that soon would fly high and fast over the Murovian Continent. He had seen the airships from afar, high in the sky, but never imagined that someday he would learn how to pilot one.

The pilot and his two passengers went aboard the flying machine. There was a belt harness in each seat and Torr was instructed as to its use. Kalac sat by the side of the pilot in front of another set of controls while Torr sat to their right facing a window. The cabin was circular with round transparent windows all around. There was a circular column from floor to ceiling in the center of the cabin.

After the pilot and Kalac checked and positioned some levers a humming noise was heard and as the sound increased the ship started to rise – to levitate. The pilot moved another set of levers and they glided forward heading for an exit tunnel; as they entered Torr saw what appeared to be a waterfall at the other end. For a moment he was shaken up, he thought they were going to crash against a waterfall but the ship went right through it and emerged unscathed on the other side, then arching upward and rapidly gathering speed vanished from view.

Amazing! Torr thought.

Hardly any clouds covered the sky and as the airship devoured time and distance, images of valleys and rolling hills materialized and vanished before their eyes. No high mountains existed in the land of Muror – only hills. The highest points: Mount Ymon in the Province of Phara, Mount Gauf in the Ayas Province and the Mount Boac Mining Complex in the Storca Region of the Oenic Province.

******

In less than half-an-hour they came within visual range of Liss, center of commerce and principal city of Muror, now illuminated by a splendorous sunset. Innumerable ribbons of golden arrows pierced the clouds bathing the city with a golden glow.

They overflew the city. Once over the bay they lost altitude and raced back heading for Kalac's house that was located in a rocky promontory that jutted out three miles into the bay. There was an opening on a ledge by one of the sides of the house; it could only be seen from the air. The pilot slowed down and hovering over the ledge guided the ship into an underground cavern; off-loading the passengers he headed back to Nalta.

There were two ships in the cavern. Kalac walked over to one of the ships and said, "This one is like the one we flew in, it is the same model you will use in your missions and the first you must learn to fly. You will also get to fly the one over there; it is much faster and capable of operating outside the planet atmosphere but we never use it when we visit or land in other countries. It is a secret technology that the Atlanteans do not have. The one that you will be flying uses the same technology as their ships so there is nothing to worry about if for some reason it falls in their hands."

"When are we leaving for the secret base?" Torr asked.

"Before sunrise tomorrow," Kalac answered. "Tonight we must pay a visit to the Sailors' Temple. I have to inform them about your transfer and you must pick up the rest of your belongings."

They went up a flight of stairs to the house; there Torr met Yamila, Kalac's wife. Yamila was a priestess and had been married to Kalac since they graduated from the Temple College. Because of body cell regeneration Kalac and Yamila looked much younger than their real age. One of the many frequencies generated by the crystal powerhouse was used for healing and body regeneration. Because of the years needed to accumulate their knowledge the keepers of esoteric and technological secrets were routinely submitted to body regeneration.

Kalac ordered that a hound-cart be brought to the front door, then accompanied Torr to the temple.

******

It was a long night for Torr; a nagging thought kept him awaked most of the night, he kept asking himself the same questions – is life pre-destined? Does the future already exist? Or, do you create your own future?

CHAPTER 4

Next dawn Kalac and Torr were on their way. Once aboard the ship Kalac did not waste any time; he explained and demonstrated how a frequency generated by a powerhouse or an on-board oscillator would bring to a boiling point the mercury in the ship propulsion system. He flipped a lever to start the engine boiling cycle. Not long after, an indicator told him that the engine was ready. Then he slowly opened a valve that controlled the flow of vaporized mercury to the vortex coils and the ship lifted off. With another set of levers he vectored the ionized air being sucked in around the vortex coil core enclosure and guided the ship out into the open sky.

Flying over the clouds heading toward the Storca Region Kalac waited until the sun came up over the horizon before asking, "What...if we start your flying lessons?"

Torr smiled and said, "I'm ready if you are."

For the next hour or so Kalac demonstrated the control inputs needed to fly the ship and Torr replicated all the maneuvers.

Reaching the Big River – the boundary between the Phara and Oenic Provinces – Kalac veered left and followed the river toward the sea in the direction of Kupol.

Eventually they encountered a large lake-shaped area in the river; the junction to Trell – another seaport north of Kupol. When the ship was over the center of the lake Kalac made a right turn heading south; then told Torr, "Mount Boac will be to our right. We have to approach the base from the east. As you know there are ongoing mining operations on the western side. Our secret base is located in the tunnels excavated on the eastern side more than 50,000 years ago. A long, long time ago, the entrances to those tunnels were sealed and the only way to enter is by air or a secret entrance you will learn about."

As they came closer to Mount Boac Torr saw why this site was selected. The mount was a cone-shaped rock about ten-miles wide with a depression in the center and rocky vertical inside walls; devoid of any vegetation. It was the highest point around, so, to any observer in the low lands it would look like if the ship overflew the mount and kept flying in a direction that could not be seen from his vantage point.

Kalac came in flying close to the rim and dropped down into the center of the depression. While hovering in place he waited for the all clear signal.

A light flashed on the panel, Kalac then positioned a lever and after a short delay the vertical wall in front of the ship parted. Entering the opening the ship was guided through a lighted tunnel that ended up in a huge cavern.

After landing Kalac shut down the engine. When they came out of the ship Torr noticed that there were so many torches illuminating the cavern that it looked like if they were outside in actual daylight. There were a lot of ships in the cavern; it seemed as if they were working on some of them, panels had been removed and Torr could see their innards.

While they walked toward the extreme end of the cavern Kalac said, "They are being checked to make sure that they are in an airworthy condition."

Going through a metal door and another tunnel they went up a long flight of stairs that led to the Base Operations Office. When they entered the room Torr saw that the walls were covered by maps of the planet and on a table he saw something that he had never seen before; it looked like a window, images of the terrain surrounding the base could be seen on flat mirrors.

The priest in the room told Kalac that he was expected and led them to the base commander office.

When they entered the office a man sitting behind a large desk stood up and looking at Kalac said, "Glad to see you again...and he, I have to assume, is our new trainee."

"Yes he is," Kalac said; then added, "Torr, this is Caleb, a High-Priest and the base commander."

"It is an honor," Torr said.

After the usual get acquainted small talk they went over the training requirements. There had never been a need for such an accelerated training so there was no curriculum available.

Flying training will be of primary importance but other subjects must also be covered; like what to expect in the regions that he may have to visit and the enhancement of his psychic capabilities.

It took more than two hours to prepare the projected timetable. Wasting no time Caleb called his assistant and giving him the document ordered that arrangements be made so that Torr could start training the next morning. Caleb then suggested to Kalac that the rest of the day he acquaint Torr with the base.

When they left Caleb's office Kalac remembered the puzzled look in Torr's face when he saw the reflected views on the table mirrors so on their way out he stopped by the mirrors and explained, "For security reasons we don't have windows to the outside. Glass fiber cables and lenses are used to reflect the outside images on the table mirrors. It is the same technology used in the magnifying screens that we have in our airships."

Torr noticed that in one set of mirrors he could see the valleys around Mount Boac and in another set the entire area inside the crater.

The priest in charge of flight operations said, "In order not to compromise the location of the base we have to make sure that nobody is around – on the rim or inside the crater.

"If all is clear I send a signal to the ship and if I get the correct identification code I'll open the door."

In one of the reflected images Torr saw a small fenced in village with a building that looked like a temple, so he asked, "What are those buildings and how come they seem to be so close to the base?"

Kalac answered, "That is where the people that work here live. As you probably figured out, the building in the center of the village is a temple. To outsiders and other residents of the village it is a temple dedicated to scroll writing. They must have told you about this place while you were in school."

"Yes, we were told that there is a temple where scroll writers generate all the written material that is needed in our schools and temples and that it was located in the Oenic Province."

Kalac added, "Near a hundred priests and priestesses are supposed to work there – one half priests and the other half priestesses, but, what the residents of the village or outsiders don't know is that the ones working as scroll writers are the priestesses. The priests work here, they are the Priest-Scientists and their assistants. The priestesses working as scroll writers are married to the priests that work here.

"The temple offers a perfect cover. Because of the confidential nature of some of the scrolls no outsider is allowed to enter the premises where the scroll writers work. Even the temple priest doesn't know and is not allowed to enter the writers' workplace."

"It is quite ingenious," Torr said, "restricting the entrance to the writers' workplace because they do some confidential work. If it was not so it would be impossible to account for the missing priests. By the way, how do the priests get here?"

Kalac answered, "There is a secret underground tunnel that leads to the base; it is five miles long. A monorail transport system like the ones used in Atlantis is used to speed up the commuting between the temple and the base."

After instructing Torr on flight operations procedures Kalac took Torr on a tour of the base and introduced him to the base personnel; the Priest-Scientists, their assistants and the priests that took care of the base maintenance and housekeeping.

The last thing Kalac did before calling it a day was to show Torr the entrance to the tunnel that led to the temple. Then both of them went back to the ship so that Torr could pick up his belongings.

Torr was escorted to the visitors' quarters and Kalac left the base and headed home.

The sun was fast disappearing over the Western horizon. For Torr, the next dawn will bring forth a new beginning – a new reality would be forged and a new time-line created.

CHAPTER 5

Iltar was ready – he called Esman and told him to come over to his office.

A knock was heard at the door.

"Come in," Iltar ordered.

It was Esman.

"Sit down," Iltar told Esman. "I have an operational plan ready and I want you to present it to the generals."

Esman asked, "Is it going to be the Naga Empire?"

"Yes, but I decided not to go for the capital of the empire," Iltar answered as he unfolded a large map of the Naga Empire (India).

"We are not going to the capital of the empire?" Esman asked with a certain tone of surprise in his voice.

"No, we are not," Iltar answered. "The configuration of their empire is similar or very close to ours; that means that they operate like independent kingdoms, therefore, each one of them can sign treaties on their own as long as the treaties do not affect the other kingdoms.

"The King of Kings that rules the empire has a larger army and can order the other kingdoms to come to his aid. They are no match for our weapons but if they have numerical superiority over our expeditionary force they may decide to put up a fight and that is not what we want."

Indicating a city on the map Iltar said, "This is where we are going first."

"Mohenjo-Daro," Esman muttered.

Iltar said, "Yes, the capital of one of the empire kingdoms."

"Are you sure that's the way?" Esman asked.

"I do," Iltar answered; then added, "I need you to meet with the generals, go over the operational plan with them; tell them to be ready to carry out the plan as soon as I convince Uranus to let us try to negotiate new protection and trade agreements.

"They must follow the procedures that I have outlined. The military strategy is up to them; but they must obey the prime directive – do not use force unless forced to do so; if that is the case the force must be directed toward their leaders."

"Will I be going with them?" Esman asked.

"No," Iltar answered.

"Then, who are we sending?" Esman inquired.

Iltar answered, "The same ambassador that dealt with Queen Moo; I already briefed him. You are going to be the liaison with the military here in Semira. Unlike you, it would be questionable if I was seen visiting the military."

After Iltar went over the operational plan with Esman he folded the map, inserted it in a satchel with the written instructions and then told Esman, "Now is up to you, go and present the plan to the generals."

Esman stood up; picked up the satchel and as he headed for the door he said, "As soon as I get back I will inform you about the outcome of the meeting."

"So be it," Iltar said.

Esman left the office; went down to the subterranean dock beneath the palace and found a boat that was about to leave for the Large Port; the location of the Military Headquarters. The subterranean channel under the palace ran all the way down to the ocean, six miles away. The Large Port was about two-thirds of the way there.

When Esman reached the Military Headquarters he went to General Darko's office and requested to see the general. Darko was in charge of the Air Assault Forces.

Once in Darko's office, after exchanging greetings, Esman said, "General, from now on I will be your contact, Iltar can't be seen visiting military installations; it would be most unusual and would be noticed. On the other hand, I'm an ambassador and one of my duties is meeting with the military to discuss military treaties. As you know, I have had dealings with you before, so my presence in your office is a logical consequence of my duties."

Esman opened the satchel; removed its contents and said, "This is the operational plan for our next venture. You have to check the mission directives and military strategy to make sure that they can be accomplished as planned."

The general reviewed the plan; the only concern he had was about the possible military response alternatives to the prime directive. Once he agreed to the plan he said, "Let's go to the base and brief General Khun and his officers."

There was a funicular station by the building so it didn't take long to board a passenger pod and be on their way. The electric powered pods hung from a monorail strung along metal poles that linked all the neighborhoods of the circular city and some of the outlying areas; like the Semira Air Base.

Huge granite mountains; with almost vertical cliffs existed to the east, south, and west of Semira.

They were heading east toward the western slope of the mountain where the air base was located – forty miles away.

In half an hour they reached their destination; the western side of the mountain. It was an impressive sight that never ceased to amaze Esman. The terraced cliffs of the tall mountain resembled a stairway; a path to the gates of heaven. The effect was uncanny; especially that day for low laying clouds covered the mountain peak.

Many thousands of years earlier, stone blocks were quarried from the surface and the interior of the mountain to embellish the buildings of Semira. It was the only quarry that could supply gray stones with black swirling patterns imbedded in them.

After many, many millenniums, it was decided that the huge caverns created by the removal of the stones could be used to protect their air transports and vailxi from the weather or possible enemy attacks. The quarry was converted to an air base – military and civilian.

Wasting no time Esman and Darko went straight to Khun's office; who after being told the reason for the visit told an office clerk to locate the junior officers and to tell them to report to the briefing room.

Esman and Darko then proceeded to familiarize Khun with the operational plan. Once the three of them agreed as to what was expected, and that it was feasible, they headed for the briefing room where they found the officers waiting; eager to find out what was happening.

The generals and Esman sat at a table. General Khun opened the satchel, removed the map, stood up, went to a board on the wall behind the table, tacked the map of the Naga Empire to the board, then as he indicated a location on the map he said, "Men, this is our objective; Mohenjo-Daro; one of the seven capital cities or Rishi-Cities of the Naga Empire.

"Before we go, Iltar will have to convince Uranus that it would be a good idea to send an ambassador on a mission beyond the Inland Sea to explore the possibility of signing new trade or protection treaties.

As soon as we get the go ahead I'll lead the mission with 300 men. We can't take along all of our Air Assault Forces; that would leave us with no fast-ground-response if we have to defend our kingdom.

"Since only three squadrons are needed only three of you will be going."

General Khun went over to the selected officers; gave each one of them a scroll and said, "That is a list of the equipment and supplies needed.

"And as for the other three of you not going please help your fellow officers get ready.

"We will use two of our cylindrical transports, each one carrying two vailxi (airships) and 150 soldiers.

"The vailxi will be catapulted from the transports one hour before we reach the landing field; they will serve as escorts and protect the transports while they land. After the transports land the vailxi will come to rest by their sides and stand on full alert while we are on the ground. I want the pilots to take turns, always one of them on watch and ready to repel any attack. I don't want any surprises.

"After landing I will accompany our ambassador to pay our respects to the Rishi-King and to request permission to stay overnight to rest and provision our ships.

"Protocol calls for the king to invite our ambassador and officers to dinner that night; at that time we will try to convince the king about the advantages of our protection treaties."

Khun then told the officers about the prime directive and why the use of force was a last resort option.

One of the officers asked, "What if we have to use force? What are we going to tell the soldiers? What about Uranus when we get back?"

Khun answered, "If we have to use force you will tell your men, or any of the king's officials when we get back, that we had to take action because we were threatened and the present trade agreement cancelled when we offered them protection from the barbaric tribes.

"Uranus will be told that we acted in self-defense and that in order to protect our interests in the region we deemed necessary to help effect a change of leadership in the kingdom by helping a priest, that shared our views, in becoming their new Rishi-King. But I don't think it will come to that. They can't refuse our offer after what we are planning on telling them.

"Our flight will take us over their Western frontier. We plan to tell them that in our way to Mohenjo-Daro we saw a barbaric tribe raiding and burning a small village on the other side of their Western frontier and that in the future those nomads may decide to cross over to raid and burn their villages.

"They have never been attacked...yet; but the truth of the matter is that there are a lot of hostile tribes out there and one day this could happen.

"Like all the other Naga Kingdoms they only have a ground army; a primitive one at that, foot soldiers equipped with bows and arrows, lances, and swords. To mobilize their troops they depend on elephants and carts. By the time they respond to an attack it would be too late.

"Once the Military Protection Treaty is signed we have to install transmitters in strategic locations along the border so that if the raiders are seen crossing over we can act before they can attack their villages or the farmlands.

"Our vailxi could be on their way within an hour after we receive the call and arrive before the invaders have time to attack the villages or the farms. With our weapons it would be an easy task to destroy the invaders. It could serve as a good training exercise for our pilots,"

Everybody laughed.

Khun continued, "Uranus and the treasury officials will be pleased if we signed such a treaty. The treasury will receive precious metals and jewels that would help to pay for our military forces."

One of the officers interrupted and asked, "How are we going to get our share? The volume and value of what we buy from them is very low."

General Khun answered, "Since our share can't be part of the value of the imports or of the official treaty we must convince the Rishi-King that it would be advisable that a specific amount – not mentioned in the treaty – should be paid, unofficially, to our military leaders; to be divided among key personnel as an incentive for a fast response.

"Now, let's talk about our time of departure, this is very important and critical; it has to be timed so that our arrival coincides with their daybreak.

"Considering the speed of our transports and that we'll be heading east we must depart at first light, and travel in our real time all day and half a night; that would position us over the landing field just about daybreak – their time. So, plan for an early morning departure.

"You will be told about the rest of the plan as we go along, meanwhile, you can start requisitioning the equipment listed in the scrolls that I gave you.

"As always, we will have daily meetings at the end of the day to check on our readiness status.

"It should not take long to get ready, but we have to wait until we get the go ahead from Uranus.

"To your soldiers or to anybody inquiring as to what is happening; it's just another training exercise."

Khun went over to the board and removed the map, then told the officers, "The meeting is adjourned. You can go back to your squadrons."

Darko and Esman returned to the Large Port. From there Esman went straight to the Royal Palace.

When Esman entered Iltar's office he noticed that Iltar seemed to be in a bad mood, so he asked, "Now what? Do we have a problem?"

Iltar answered, "Our plans will be delayed at least twenty days. I was unable to contact Uranus; he was not feeling well so he retired to his mountain retreat and left word not to be disturbed under any circumstances. If my memory serves me right when that happens he stays there for twenty to thirty days, and he really means it when he says not to be disturbed under any circumstances.

"It is true that he leaves the running of the country to us but the approval of what we are suggesting is out of our competence."

Esman gave an account of what had transpired during the meeting with the generals; then summarized it by saying, "Everything seems to be going according to plan, except of course for the delay."

"That's good to know," Iltar said, "but at this moment there is nothing that we can do but wait, I'll call the generals and tell them to put everything on hold."

"So be it," Esman said as he left the office; he left thinking that a few days wouldn't make any difference.

CHAPTER 6

It was Torr's first day of training. While he waited for the instructors it finally dawned on him that there was no turning back. Was he destined to create or change events that would alter the world historical time-line? Maybe, maybe not, but of one thing he was sure, in this life he would never be what he envisioned – a simple temple priest.

In the next thirty days they will teach him the basics; of special importance, the flying of the airships. It takes years of training to become a Priest-Scientist.

Torr heard footsteps, it was the instructors. They exchanged greetings with Torr.

As soon as they sat down the older priest said, "We will be your instructors for the next thirty days, my name is Ku and I will enhance your psychic powers and familiarize you with the places you will have to visit," and looking toward his younger companion said, "His name is Thek, he will instruct you in the universal sciences. Also will be your flight instructor.

"A lot of information must be covered in a short time, so let us begin. You are already familiar with our teaching methods so we will start as soon as the projectors are set."

Ku went over to where Thek was setting up the machines and Torr sat facing a white screen where words and images would be projected.

When everything was ready Thek said, "We will start from the beginning, the creation of the matrix of space-time and matter. It will be an abridged explanation, just enough to help you understand the scientific and esoteric concepts that you will be dealing with. The visualization of the structure of matter is very important in the comprehension of the universal forces that you will learn to control."

Thek flipped a lever turning the projectors on.

A rhythmic low steady drumbeat mixed with musical notes filled the room.

By synchronizing Torr's heartbeat with the steady beat of the drum they slowed down his body rhythm making his mind receptive to learning.

Writing and drawings will be projected on the screen, timed to concord with a recording.

And so Torr's quest began, the first lesson was now in progress. A recording was heard synchronized with the pictures being shown.

UNIVERSAL GENESIS

In the beginning, before time, space or matter existed; God existed as an uncreated source; co-existing with eternity.

Possessing self-awareness and free will God dwell in the midst of a continuous static field of energy. A field of primal energy (spirit) generated by His awareness of being.

Because of a lack of events or points of receptivity (the energy field was static and represented unity) we can say that God dwell in a condition of non-being as perceived from our space-time frame, a situation that can represent eternity.

An event (since it must have a beginning and an end or points of receptivity) can't be eternal, but a condition (unitary static condition) can represent eternity.

At some point God decided to give creative expression to His thoughts. For this to happen He needed to disturb the energy field to create events and points of receptivity so that an electrical picture-play of all He could imagine could be generated upon a matrix.

The light or vibrational energy that flowed from the focal point of God's consciousness was felt by the energy field, the result was the separation or tearing apart of two flat-linear layers of the energy field. As the layers recede the energy field must be encapsulated so that it can define points of receptivity. As the layers recede away from each other more psychic energy must be continuously encapsulated; this is accomplished by the 'Basic Frequency of Creation'. The frequency waves that are created are imprinted in the cord-like links that bridge the points of rupture; they vibrate like cords in a musical instrument.

A clockwise vortex-like wave is generated from the points of receptivity toward the peripheral center of the interval where they oppose each other enclosing and spinning the encapsulated energy field.

The encapsulated field is ball-shaped and there are seven dimensional layers to fill the voids; each one of the layers another dimensional universe, each one interlaced with the other.

The universe was not created from a single point but from a linear flat tear in the energy field. This is why it is impossible to find a single point of creation.

Flat layers of energy are still being encapsulated as the tear expands.

The encapsulated energy field interval becomes the matrix of space – ether particles.

At the same time that God is creating the matrix (ether particles) He creates the seven main divisions of the spiritual realm, the souls, and the etheric patterns needed to generate the electrical picture-play that will conform to His creative vision.

The ether particles only respond to vibrations or light waves generated by etheric patterns.

From the ether particles God creates the basic elements needed to create not only our physical universe but other inter-dimensional universes, universes that because of their vibrations and relative mass are beyond our physical perception.

Of our perceived universe, the first physical particle created was the neutron. The vibratory frequency of its etheric pattern agglutinated many ether particles to form a clump that creates a neutral particle – the neutron.

Another pattern, the proton-etheric-pattern modulated the neutron-etheric-pattern, forcing the neutron to eject a clump of its particles, this clump becomes the electron. The neutron becomes a proton.

Now we have a clump of particles called a proton and a clump called the electron.

The proton, due to the neutron-etheric-pattern will try to revert back to what it was; a neutron, but, a proton pattern and a modulating hydrogen-etheric-pattern will prevent that from happening. Timing of the three patterns is such that it will generate a cycle of attraction-repulsion-attract..., as a consequence, the electron will jump around in an oscillating path circling the proton. We end up with the building block of our universe – the hydrogen atom.

All the elements were created the same way as the hydrogen atom.

A low-level soul-pattern is involved in the creation of the elements, for all matter in the universe, to exist, must be aware of itself.

Everything else is created by high-level or mid-level soul-patterns.

The soul-pattern is the cohesive force that shapes, gives life to the object; it is the blueprint of what God envisions.

Next, we are going to cover the basics of gravitational fields so that you'll be able to understand how the engine in the airship works.

Free ether particles are everywhere, in-between atoms and inside the atoms, and because of their small size they are free to enter and leave the atoms, but their mobility is somewhat restricted by the circling electron clumps and the nucleus. The more clumps circling the nucleus the harder it is for the ether particles to penetrate or leave the atom; this is due to the speed of the circling electron clumps, they act as a porous membrane, almost like a solid shell in the case of very dense atoms.

Gravitational fields are generated by the master- etheric-patterns that create the object body. How? The free ether particles inside the atoms are oscillated toward the center of the dense body by the object master-etheric-pattern. The duration of the pulse, or frequency, is made to coincide with the time it would take for the free ether particles inside the atoms to try to exit the atom and to strike the nucleus and the circling shells. This will transfer inertial forces in the direction of the oscillation; the center of the object body. Even our bodies have a gravitational field; a very small one at that, but still there.

Now that you have a basic understanding of what gravity is we can explain how our repulsion drives work. This is the type of power plant used on the ship that can fly out of the atmosphere and that you must also learn to fly in case you have to use it to accomplish your mission.

A drawing of the innards of the airship was projected on the screen. A segmented metallic disk inside the perimeter of the round ship was highlighted and part of the drawing showed a cross-section of the metallic disk.

As you can surmise, there are a huge number of layers of atoms in that metallic disc. To achieve repulsion, to cancel gravity, we oscillate the ether particles inside the atoms so that they transfer their inertia to the nucleus and the electron shells of the atoms in the metallic disk.

The oscillation frequency is applied to the atomic layers in a sequential order, bottom to top. The frequency generated by crystal oscillators.

The pulse is applied during the relax portion of the master-etheric-pattern vibration cycle that creates the massive object that we want to repel off from; and in the opposite direction to the massive object center of mass.

When all the segments of the disk are aligned in a horizontal position, parallel to the earth surface, the ship will levitate. To travel in a specific direction, segments of the metal disc are rotated to change the direction of the resultant forces.

The first lesson was over – Thek stopped the machines; then asked, "Is everything understood?"

"Yes," Torr answered.

"Great," Thek said. "Now, let's take a look at a ship."

The next step was to familiarize Torr with the ship that he was going to use on his missions; the one with the mercury power plant.

They went over to the hangar; there they found a ship that had all of its service panels removed. Torr was able to see the ship mechanical systems while Thek explained their function and operational relevance with respect to the ship controls.

Ku had been tagging along all this time; one of his duties was to supervise Torr's training.

The first flying lesson was to take place later that afternoon, but now, it was lunch time, so they headed for the dining hall; most of the base personnel were there but Kalac wasn't. Torr hadn't seen him since the previous night so he asked Thek, "Where is Kalac? I have not seen him today."

Thek answered, "I was told that he went to Nalta. There was something about your mission that he had to clear with the Archpriest."

After lunch Torr was told to take a half-an-hour break before reporting back to the classroom. He decided to take a closer look at the base facilities so he wandered around the base. As he went by the exit-entry tunnel he saw it again and wondered what was on the other side of the white door. They had shown him everything, including the tunnel that led to the village, but nobody ever mentioned what was behind that door. It was a huge sliding door the same size as the exit-entry tunnel. Probably a storage room, Torr thought.

With the lunch break over, it was time to return to the classroom.

******

Meanwhile, at Nalta, Kalac was telling the Archpriest, "I need your approval on something that must be done if the mission is to be a success.

"As you are aware, it is certain that eventually Torr will have to go to Semira and there is no safe place near Semira to land and hide the ship. The only safe place is in our secret outpost in the Northwest Mountains, and there are only seven of us that know its location; or that it exists!

"There is something else, Torr is not familiar with their technical devices or the city layout and commuter system; for that reason I'm recommending that for the first two days he be accompanied by the outpost priest. After two days he should be able to be on his own.

"Do you approve my plan? Can we use the outpost?"

The Archpriest hesitated for a moment then said, "Well, if there is no other alternative it must be done the way you propose, but, I want to talk to him the moment he finishes his training,"

"Of course," Kalac said. "I'll bring him to see you the moment he is ready to go.

"Tomorrow I will tell Caleb about what we just decided. Now I'm going home."

The meeting was over. The Archpriest left the room and Kalac returned to his ship.

******

Torr found the instructors waiting for him when he returned to the classroom. As soon as he sat down Thek said, "Our next lesson will deal with the ship capabilities and how the ship controls affect the flight directional changes.

"At the end of the class we will take you out for your first flying lesson. Kalac told us that on your way here he let you handle the ship; that should help for you already experienced how the ship behaves to control movements; now you will learn why and how is this accomplished by the ship systems."

******

The next two hours were spent learning about systems, instruments, and flying techniques. When they felt that Torr was ready they went over to the hangar where they presented him with a brand new ship – his ship; the one that he would be flying from now on; for training and for his covert operations.

After a walk-around inspection they went aboard. Torr did the usual pre-flight checks and then initiated the engine boiling cycle. When the ready light came on Torr positioned some levers and the ship left the ground, then, Thek guided Torr's control inputs as he went through the tunnel. Once outside they let him handle the controls by himself, and as instructed headed east.

When the ship cleared the rim of Mount Boac it kept flying parallel to the ground for about ten miles; then, in a burst of speed it reached out for the sky; once there, above the clouds, a choreographed dance began. All possible maneuvers were performed by Thek; and Torr replicated them.

For more than an hour they kept at it, dancing all over the sky, but the inexorable rotation of the planet was about to put an end to the flying spectacle for the sun was fast approaching the Western horizon – it was time to return to the base. So, Thek said, "Let's go back, but before you approach the base from the east I want you to fly parallel to Mount Boac on the south side, there is something I want to show you."

"And what would that be?"

Thek answered, "I want you to see where the miners that work in the mines live. The village is not visible from the base – it is surrounded by hills. Close by, on the other side of the village is where the ores are smelted and the jewelry manufacturing industries are located."

After a fleeting look of the village they returned to the base, just before the sun disappeared over the horizon. The first flying lesson was over.

Thek and Ku went back to the village, and Torr, after getting something to eat retired to his living quarters.

******

On the second day, following a class on navigation they went flying.

This time Torr will find out what the ship was capable of; to explore the outer limits; maximum speed and altitude.

Torr followed the same route as the previous day and when about ten miles out was told to head for Kupol – at maximum speed. Kupol was the largest seaport on the East coast of the Murovian Continent.

It didn't take long to get there. Once over the city Torr was directed away from the coastal area; to head out over the ocean.

When Thek considered that they were at a safe distance from land he ordered, "Now, go down and position the ship twenty feet over the ocean surface."

"Yes, I see what your intentions are," Torr said, "and I suspect that this is not going to be as easy as when it is done at a higher altitude."

"You are quite right," Thek said. "At that low altitude you must concentrate, think ahead of the ship and be on the lookout for any obstacles in your flight path. The automatic guidance system will maintain the altitude but you must be ready to go to manual control and take evasive action if an obstruction appears in the flight path."

The moment Torr positioned the ship over the ocean Thek said, "Let's do it, now...maximum speed."

Torr complied with the order. As the ship accelerated – because of the deflected air – it left behind a turbulent wake of foamy water over the ocean surface.

It was an exhilarating experience, at high altitude you hardly notice the speed, but now, close to the ocean surface the horizon was coming at you at a fantastic rate of speed.

Torr remembered that the other ship was supposed to be much faster and he imagined how it would be to fly that ship at this low altitude at maximum speed.

After doing a few high speed runs Thek said, "Let's take the ship to its maximum ceiling so that you can feel how the controls behave at that altitude. As you know, the vortex coil doesn't need air to operate, but to hover and maintain a stable position ionized air has to be ejected from the rim to have precise directional control."

Torr stopped the ship forward motion and started a vertical ascent. When they reached an altitude of thirty miles Thek said, "Stop, now try hovering, try to hold the ship steady in place and then move forward."

The ship experienced a slight wobble; its behavior was not as precise as when at a lower altitude when changing its heading because of the lower volume of ionized atmosphere.

Torr was then ordered to descent and to return to the base, they have to be back by noon. For the rest of the day Torr will be back in the classroom.

******

The afternoon lesson will be imparted by Ku; the subject matter; levitation.

Ku began by telling Torr, "As a covert operator this will be one of your principal assets, one day you might have to use it to save your life or to reach places that others can't.

33

"Not everybody can master levitation to its full extent for you must be able to maintain and hold your visualization while performing a task; not many people can do it.

"There is a similarity in achieving levitation and how the engine of our anti-gravity ship works; in both cases inertial forces are transmitted to the nucleus and the circling electron shell(s) of the atoms.

"The planet master-etheric-pattern vibrations attract the ether particles inside the atoms of your body toward the nucleus of the planet. This transfer of inertial forces toward the nucleus of the planet is what keeps you on the planet surface.

"The planet master-etheric-pattern vibrations consist of – ON...OFF...ON...OFF..., pulses. On the OFF portion of the planet pulse the etheric-patterns of the individual atoms will return the ether particles to their previous state; back in equilibrium.

"If during the OFF portion of the planet pulse you were to visualize the ether particles being pulsed in the opposite direction – away from the planet nucleus – then you can achieve levitation.

"The planet master-etheric-pattern vibrates at a frequency close to eight times during the time you blink an eye. You will be shown how to control your breathing rate and to generate a frequency that will oppose the planet frequency so that you can neutralize the planet gravity field.

"The first thing you must learn is how to concentrate, and we mean really concentrate. Using deep hypnosis we will implant in your mind the phrase ENZAZIL. From then on every time you voice the phrase you will enter a state of deep concentration that can't be broken unless you voice the phrase again. While under this state of concentration you will be fully aware of your surroundings, you will be in full control and whatever is happening around you will not break your concentration; while under this state you must constantly generate in your mind the secret syllable that we'll tell you about, and at the same time visualize a stream of light pulses entering your navel and exiting at the top of your head.

"You don't have to voice the syllable, whenever you think, your larynx vibrates repeating your thoughts, and since the larynx is in the path – a direct line – between the top of your head and your navel it will modulate the light pulses in the visualized path.

"There is one other thing you must be familiar with before we go ahead – the propagation of light waves; it would help in visualizing the stream of light pulses entering your body.

"When vibrations create heat the hydrogen atoms in space are raised to a higher energy state and their equilibrium is altered; the hydrogen master-etheric-pattern that created the atom tries to bring it back to its primal state; when it does so, the energy generated in returning the atom to its primal state is then transferred to the adjacent atom, and so on...

"The hydrogen master-etheric-pattern is what allows the transfer of energy between celestial bodies. For example, the sun heats our planet atmosphere.

"Are there any questions before we proceed?"

"No...All is understood," Torr answered.

"If you are ready, let's start," Ku said; then went over to the projectors and turned them on.

The steady beats of the drums were heard......

CHAPTER 7

Queen Moo decided that it was time; time to leave Sais and to return to Mayax; but before doing so there was a place that she wanted to visit. That night at the dinner table, with Thoth and Chronus present, she asked Thoth, "When is the next caravan leaving for the Naga settlements?"

"I believe in a few days," Thoth answered; then asked, "Are you planning on visiting them?"

"Yes," Queen Moo replied. "I would like to meet with the leaders of the Maioo settlement before I go back home. Can you arrange passage for me and my maids on the next caravan leaving Sais?"

"Yes, of course, consider it done," Thoth replied.

"What if I take you there in my vailx?" Chronus asked.

"I appreciate your offer," Queen Moo answered, "but on my way there I want to be able to observe the fauna of the region – at ground level!"

Thoth and Chronus laughed when she said – at ground level! They knew she was afraid of flying.

While at Sais Queen Moo never tried to ask Chronus about the military treaties; but now she saw the opportunity – in a roundabout way – to see if he had anything to do with the treaties, so she asked Chronus, "Is the Maioo Colony protected by your military treaties?"

"Not as far as I know," Chronus answered. "Of course I have been away for about three months. If anything has changed I'm not aware of it. I don't get involved in such matters. After Uranus approval it's up to the ambassadors and generals to negotiate the treaties."

That's all Queen Moo needed to know, it was evident that Chronus didn't know what was going on. This must be a military extortion plot, most likely a corrupt general and a few other rouge officials, like an ambassador. She must find out how many were involved before deciding what to do.

After the meal the three of them were joined by Thoth's wife who had been looking after her daughter – Misar. They headed for the ceremonial center-court of the temple. The temple orchestra was playing that night.

Once seated the magic unfolded as the virtuosos played. The music generated by the instruments imitated a medley of planetary vibrations – the enchanting voices of nature. It was the voice of God emulated by one of his creations – man.

Once the symphony was over they retired for the night.

******

Three days later Queen Moo and her maids were on their way; they left Sais before dawn and now were aboard a boat headed for the junction where the Nile River branches out to form the delta.

Pushed by a strong wind the sailboat seemed to glide over the river surface. A flock of birds swooped over the river looking for their daily sustenance. Once in a while a bird will dive and with its claws snag a fish from the water – the food chain being orchestrated. The rising sun made the ripples on the river surface sparkle with a twinkling cadence as the boat made its way upriver. To their left on the high ground the cultivated fields, and on their right; marshes.

******

All day the boat raced with the wind; it reached the delta station ahead of schedule. That night they would stay at the station inn.

******

At daybreak they resumed their journey; this time they will travel on the overland trail, riding on wagons. Four of the wagons were loaded with trade goods; another one carried four passengers, and Queen Moo and her maids in a wagon by themselves. The Trail Master in the lead wagon with the daily supplies and the emergency equipment.

Every night; for the next three days, they would spent the night at a relay station.

On the fourth day they reached the Red Sea Gulf Port.

******

The next day they were on their way again, this time aboard an ocean-going ship heading south. Their next stop will be the Maioo outpost; a small Naga settlement.

CHAPTER 8

Torr was about to start his last week of training. As soon as he entered the classroom Ku told him, "There is much to be done so let's start. I want you to concentrate and while we speak try to levitate."

Torr proceeded to do so.

Ku did the same.

As they faced each other Ku told Torr, "You have mastered the subject matter; there is no need to practice anymore. So, I must remind you that you can't let others see you doing it, unless it's done to save your life."

"Yes, I know," Torr said; then asked, "How many of us can do it?"

"Only the Priest-Scientists, Kalac, the Archpriest and the Arch Priestess can do it." Ku answered.

Ku then started to descend and Torr followed. Once on the ground Ku said, "You have mastered levitation, so from now on we will concentrate on the other lessons: the sensing of objects in complete darkness and in the stopping of time; once mastered they will help in your covert operations."

Torr was being trained to sense the heat radiated by organic matter; with the skin of his face – while in complete darkness! Also on how to stop time, that is, how to freeze somebody's consciousness for a short period of time – for the time it takes to slowly close and open your eyes.

The sound machines were turned on. Once again Torr's mind must be conditioned to accept what seemed to be an impossible reality.

The training went on for the rest of the morning.

******

Right after lunch Kalac took over; he told Torr, "We have taught you everything we know about the places that you may have to visit; their customs, language differences and how they dress.

"This afternoon we'll visit the temple and the village so that you can meet the villagers and see where you will reside when you finish your present training and are assigned to the temple as a scribe.

"To the villagers you will be just another scribe that works in the temple – so, let's go."

Torr followed Kalac; when they reached the tunnel entrance that leads to the temple Kalac rotated one of the small ornaments on the stone wall and the wall slid open.

The entrance was so narrow that a person could barely squeeze by.

Torr asked, "Is the entrance on the other side this narrow?"

"Yes," Kalac answered.

"Why?" Torr asked.

"For security reasons," Kalac explained. "If the village is attacked and the temple is captured we can easily seal off the doors on both sides of the tunnel by releasing a stone from the top of the entrance cubicle so that the doors are sealed off. The opening mechanism is also deactivated on both sides."

"I see," Torr said; then asked, "Can the stones be easily returned to their original operational position?"

"Yes," Kalac answered. "The mechanism can be operated in reverse, but the activating levers are not located by the doors and a sequential operation has to be performed in different locations for the mechanism to function."

On the other side of the narrow entrance, on a wide tunnel, Torr saw two overhead tracks; four pods hung from each one of them. Using one of the electric pods they reached the temple in about ten minutes.

Opening the secret door they found themselves in a basement; a storage area; from there they went up to the scribes' work area.

When Kalac entered the workroom, with a stranger, the priestesses stopped working.

One of the priestesses asked, "Is he the new trainee?"

"Yes he is and his name is Torr," Kalac answered.

Then, the Head Priestess said, "We know that you are staying at the base and that at present you are single. I need to know if you are planning on getting married when they finish your house and you move to the village; it will determine how many work stations are needed. In your case I have to set up a fake station to account for your presence. So, tell me, are you going to be married?"

Torr hesitated before answering, unpleasant memories flooded his mind, "I was to be married; she was a member of my study group and was selected to be a priestess. Two weeks before we were to graduate we went sailing. The boat capsized...her body never surfaced and was never found."

"Sorry I asked," the Head Priestess apologized.

"Don't be," Torr said. "I have accepted God's will, but I'm sorry that she had to die so that I can fulfill my destiny."

"How is that so?" the Head Priestess asked.

"We were to be assigned to the temple in the city of Barb; they needed a priest and a priestess. Because of her death I ended up at Liss where they only needed a priest.

"On my way to Nalta to participate in the athletic games I met Kalac. Because of different travel schedules I would have never met Kalac had I been assigned to the temple in the city of Barb – I wouldn't be here."

There was a long silence, Kalac then said, "Let's show you around. Follow me."

As they walked across the room Torr noticed that there were about one hundred work stations – half of them empty.

The windows faced a courtyard. On the other side of the yard: a restroom, a kitchen, a dining room, and a sitting room; the reason for all this; the priestesses can't leave their work place during their lunch time; because if that was the case, the Priest-Scientists would also have to do so and a lot of time would be wasted traveling back and forth.

After showing Torr that side of the building Kalac went over to the door; the one that separates the rest of the temple from the scribes' work area, then he told Torr, "This is the door used to access the other side of the temple and the village. Besides myself, the Archpriest and the Arch Priestess the only others allowed to enter are the scribes."

"Can we see the other side of the temple?" Torr asked.

Kalac answered, "I'm afraid not from here, there may be somebody on the other side. We didn't come in from that side of the temple. If we are seen going out from this side it wouldn't take a genius to figure out that there is another entrance; that would jeopardize our secret base. You will see it when we visit the village. So, let's get back to the base and use your ship, it's time you check out your new home and get to know some of the villagers."

Back at the base they went straight for Torr's ship; once aboard, with Torr at the controls they headed for the village; as soon as he cleared the crater Kalac told him to maintain the eastern heading. At a safe distance – out of visual range of the village – Kalac told Torr to fly north all the way to the Big River. When they reached the Big River Torr was told to make a left turn and to intercept the affluent that led to the village. At the affluent he followed its course upstream.

Once over the village Kalac pointed out, "There! To your left, the landing pad."

"Yes, I see it," Torr acknowledged.

After hovering for a short time – observing the village layout – Kalac took over the controls, he didn't want somebody noticing that Torr was sitting in the pilot's seat while they landed. Kalac landed and shut down the engine.

When they came out of the ship they saw a man walking toward the landing pad, he wore a white tunic; it was the village priest.

The priest approached the visitors and greeted them; then addressing Torr said, "You must be the new scribe for whom we are building a house."

"Yes he is; his name is Torr," Kalac answered; then added, "We are here so that he can take a look at his new home, the village, and what would be his workplace."

"Of course, follow me," the village priest said. "He must be eager to see his new home and workplace."

They followed the priest to the house. It was a typical Murovian dwelling with thick stone walls and a center courtyard. After checking out the construction progress they headed for the temple.

At the temple Kalac went directly to the door that led to the security door corridor. The security door was located at the end of the corridor.

Unlike the secret access doors that were disguised as solid stone walls this door looked like a regular door. But as Kalac demonstrated, only if you knew the sequential code could you open it – five actuators had to be positioned in a sequential order for the door to open.

Kalac opened the door and they entered the forbidden side of the temple. They stayed for a reasonable time to give the impression that Kalac was showing Torr what would be his workplace, then they returned to where the village priest was waiting. Like the rest of the villagers, the village priest was not allowed to go beyond the door that led to the corridor where the security door was located.

The rest of the day was spent in learning about the village infrastructure and in getting to know some of the residents.

At the end of the day they went back to the ship and retracing their flight path returned to the base.

Kalac; as usual, flew back home.

******

Kalac was back at first light. This time he wanted to take Torr flying before clouds started to cover the Murovian Continent.

As they approached the ships Kalac told Torr, "Today we are not using your ship. We'll use one with a gravitational repulsion power plant. I want you to see the continent from outer space; that would help you to visualize how the land features are interrelated so that you can orient yourself when flying at a lower altitude in your ship."

Kalac went directly to the selected ship; after a walk around preflight inspection they went aboard.

Before Torr could turn on the frequency generators Kalac reminded him, "You have already been checked out on this ship but not at the altitude that we'll be going, and so, I must remind you that this time you must activate the radiation shield. As you know this ship have two outer skin layers – that includes the windows. A gas is trapped between those layers. A long time ago we discovered that to protect our bodies from radiation if we go beyond a certain distance from the planet all we had to do was to shield the ship with a frequency equal to that generated by a lightning bolt; the gas contained within the two outer layers of the ship skin is oscillated at that frequency. Eventually you will learn how it is done, but now there is some flying to be done. So, activate the frequency generators and take the ship out."

Torr complied and as soon as they reached a prudent distance away from the crater Kalac ordered, "Take us up in a vertical ascent but don't use maximum power."

"Hang on...here we go," Torr said.

The ship started its vertical ascent and the continent of Muror seemed to collapse under the ship.

"Keep climbing," Kalac ordered. "Go up to an altitude of 200 miles."

"Did I hear you right? Did you say 200 miles?" Torr questioned what he just heard.

"Yes, 200 miles," Kalac reiterated.

When they reached the requested altitude Kalac said, "Now stop and turn off the frequency generators that control the artificial gravity system and the propulsion system."

Torr carried out the order. The ship now in orbit started to drift with respect to the Murovian Continent.

Kalac released his safety harness and floated away from his seat. Torr was told to do likewise. After a short time they returned to their seats and Kalac activated the gravity generators; then said, "Engage the propulsion frequency generator, stabilize the ship and hold it in place."

Torr carried out the order. The ship held its position and stopped drifting.

While they observed the ground below Kalac mentioned that the difference between the two ships was the radiation shield and their propulsion systems; except for that, both have identical systems; that is, identical atmospheric shields, artificial gravity systems and a fully automated electromechanical system that protects the occupant during abrupt changes in speed or direction.

Another plus that Kalac emphasized, their controls; the two ships have the same response rate to the control inputs.

Kalac decided that it was time to show Torr the road to Atlantis, and this seemed the perfect occasion. From their altitude he could see the clear weather patterns over the Atlantic Ocean. So, he told Torr, "There is something that I have to show you. We'll be flying out-of-range of the eight crystal towers frequency waves so make sure the on-board crystal oscillators are operational."

When Torr finished the functional check of the crystal oscillators Kalac said, "Let's head for Mayax. I want to be at an altitude of twenty-miles when we get there. Start a gradual descent as you move forward and select a speed that will position us over their capital in a quarter-of-an-hour.

"Check the maps for the coordinates of their capital."

Torr checked his navigational display, entered the coordinates and then headed for Zahia; the capital of Mayax. Half way there a light on the instrument panel flashed on, the on-board generators were taking over.

******

A quarter-of-an-hour after leaving Murovian air space they were over Zahia at an altitude of twenty-miles. While hovering in place Torr used the magnifying screen to survey the city. Kalac waited a reasonable time then ordered Torr to plot a course that would position the ship over the westernmost lands of Poseidia-Atlantis, to stay at the present altitude and to select a speed that would get them there in half-an-hour.

Torr calculated the new flight plan then guided the ship in the direction of Poseidia. On their way there they flew over an Atlantean outpost (in the Bimini area) and as they did so Kalac said, "Don't fly over this place in the other ship, unless there is no other alternative; but, if you have to do so, fly high, out of reach of their sensors. The danger would be that if by any chance their vailxi (fighters) are flying and they see you, you can't outrun them. Two vailxi are stationed there, so stay away."

******

When they reached the Northwest region of Poseidia Torr was ordered to stop and hold the ship in place; when he did so Kalac said, "I want you to pay close attention to this region, of special interest; the approach from the north; from the ocean to the valley between the high peaks. If you ever need to visit Semira I will explain during your mission briefing why you should be concerned about this area."

They were lucky, even though it was late in the afternoon there were not that many clouds and Torr had a good view of what he needed to see. Dusk was fast reaching that region of the planet so Kalac told Torr, "Find your way back to the base and plan on flying at least 200 miles away from the Atlantean outpost. Stay at the same altitude and select a speed that would take us back to the base in close to one-hour."

******

Three-quarters-of-an-hour went by and the outline of the continent of Muror appeared over the horizon. It was midmorning when they landed.

Torr was told to report back to the classroom and to be ready to go flying again in six-hours.

******

Late that afternoon they were on their way again. Torr was at the controls. As soon as they were at a safe distance from the crater Kalac said, "Let's head west, plot a course for the Inland Sea Delta and the city of Sais; plan to fly at the same altitude and speed as this morning."

The ship chased the sun. Kalac wanted to reach Sais just before dawn; that way Torr would be able to observe if there were any discernible landmarks that could orient him if a night landing was needed in future missions.

It didn't take long to be over a large chain of islands (the Philippines) and not long after that the outline of a continent appeared over the horizon; it was the southernmost region of the Uighur Empire; they overflew it and entered Naga airspace.

While over Naga territory their flight path took them over its capital and Torr using the magnifying screen was able to take a fast look at the city.

Then...daylight turned into darkness.

When they reached Sais darkness still prevailed over that region of the planet; that gave Torr a chance to orient himself relative to the river branch that converged with the Inland Sea.

From their altitude they could see the approaching arc of light as it moved across the land creating new dawns along the way.

"What an amazing view!" Torr exclaimed.

"Yes indeed," Kalac said. "I still remember the first time that I saw it from this altitude."

After a short wait the whole delta gradually became visible; then Kalac said, "Go down to ten miles, I want you to take a closer look at the terrain around Sais."

Torr asked, "Can they detect our ship?"

"No," Kalac answered. "They don't have a military outpost here. In any case, if we are sighted and they send a ship to investigate, with our speed, we can disappear from view in a blink of an eye; that will not be the case with the ship that you will be flying on your missions. So keep that in mind."

"I certainly will," Torr said; then took the ship down to the requested altitude; once there Kalac told him, "You can see that all the land around Sais including the western side of the river is under cultivation – and the land is flat. The marshes on the western bank of the river are too narrow and they lie by the cultivated land. There is no way that we can land and hide a ship close to Sais."

"Then...where?" Torr asked.

Kalac answered, "There is an uninhabited region on the west side of the river, a large swamp close to the seashore; you can see it from here. Let's head that way and see if we can find a spot where you can hide a ship."

As the ship started its forward motion toward the swamp Torr was told to position the ship about two miles west of the river and two miles from the seashore.

Once in position Kalac told him, "Drop down to tree top level; and when you do it, do it fast. If an object moves across a plane at a relative fast speed an observer doesn't have time to judge the relative position of the event."

Torr wasted no time taking the ship down; then Kalac told him, "Start flying in a spiral pattern spreading out from this spot, and watch out for the tree tops."

They started circling, gradually increasing the radius of the circles. About half-a-mile from where they started they found what they were after; a small clearing devoid of trees and what appeared to be dry land.

Kalac asked, "What do you think?"

Torr replied, "It seems as if we found the place, but if I land there how do I get out?

Kalac had a big laugh; then told Torr, "Don't worry, there is a way. First we must mark the spot, and then I will explain. Let's drop a homing beacon on this spot so that you can find the place in the dark."

Kalac operated a lever and a projectile that looked like the tip of a lance was ejected from the ship with such a velocity that it penetrated the ground disappearing below the surface.

With the beacon in place Kalac said, "The beacon is not active now, you must activate it whenever needed. So, let's see if it is operational. Activate it."

The beacon worked as expected, then Kalac said, "Take the ship straight up; ten miles, and hold it in place over the beacon."

Torr positioned the ship as ordered.

Then, Kalac said, "Let's take a look at the possible access routes."

After observing the ground on the magnifying screen Kalac said, "Sais is about a hundred miles from the river docks. You have to walk to the river docks from the landing site; about four miles. At the river docks you can secure passage for Sais in a river boat."

Torr interrupted and asked, "That sounds reasonable. But, we have a problem. How about the swamp? I have to get to the seashore so that I can walk to the docks. How deep is that water?"

"Be patient, I was getting there," Kalac said. "To reach the seashore you will use an inflatable boat."

"An inflatable what? Did you say boat?" Torr asked.

"Yes, an inflatable boat."

Torr then said, "Never heard of such a thing."

Kalac explained, "Hardly anybody knows about them; only the priests at the base and the Archpriest pilots. We carry one in each one of the ships. It is a simple design; a narrow platform to keep the occupants afloat long enough till they can be rescued. It will serve our purpose. It is stored with the survival gear. We mentioned the survival gear compartment during your classroom lessons but didn't cover in detail what it contains. Make sure that you check its contents before you leave on your first mission.

"Now...back to the boat. Once that you reach solid ground – the seashore – you must deflate it, fold it, hide it, and activate its homing beacon so that it will be easy to find when you get back.

"Once there, at the seashore, you must walk about two miles to reach the river docks."

Kalac turned off the beacon and told Torr, "Take us back to the base; you have seen all you need to see.

"The sun will be over the horizon by the time that we reach the base. This will be your first night landing."

Torr plotted the new course and headed home, now with the sun at their back.

******

As they approached the Murovian continent they saw it again; the arc of light; but this time creating darkness as it moved toward them.

When they overflew the city of Tuin the continent was already plunged into darkness.

The rest of the trip they relied on the automatic guidance system. When they reached the crater they dropped straight down and waited for the tunnel secret door to open. The approach to the base for a night landing differed from that of a day landing for obvious reasons; visibility.

They landed, secured the ship and called it a day.

Kalac as usual flew back home.

As Torr headed for his living quarters it finally dawned upon him; he had been in outer-space! He had been closer to God and to the stars; a day to remember.

CHAPTER 9

Back at Semira word came down from the King's Mountain Retreat that Uranus was about to return to Semira.

Upon hearing the news Iltar called Esman to his office and told him, "I imagine you have heard Uranus is coming back; as soon as he is back I will request an audience to get his approval. We can inform the generals that they can start requisitioning the equipment and supplies needed."

"What if Uranus doesn't approve? Esman asked.

"I'm sure he will," Iltar answered.

"But what if he doesn't?" Esman questioned; then said, "I suggest that we don't tell the generals until we get the approval."

"Hmm..., well, I think you have a point there," Iltar said. "So let's wait, after all, what are a few more days."

After a short pause Iltar said, "Another thing, we have to start planning Chronus accident."

"I've been giving it some thought," Esman said; then asked, "Do you know anything about blowing up a vailx? I think not...neither do I. It is obvious that we need a mechanic and General Khun to go ahead with our plan."

"Yes, I figured out that much," Iltar said. "General Khun will have to be the intermediary; he is familiar with the base personnel and we need somebody from the maintenance crew to do what we have in mind.

"Whatever is done to the ship has to be done in such a way that if the ship is ever recovered it won't be detected; it has to appear that it was an accident.

"As for General Darko and the other officers; we can't tell them what our true intentions are."

"I agree about not telling the others," Esman said; then asked, "What about the mechanic that will sabotage the ship? We don't want loose ends."

"Well, General Khun will have to deal with that," Iltar said; then asked, "Does the general have a sailboat?"

"I believe so," Esman answered.

"That will be perfect," Iltar said. "As soon as the vailx is sabotaged he can invite the mechanic to do some repair work on his boat. After the work is done they will go sailing – to make sure that the repair is holding up – with the misfortune that the mechanic will fall overboard and be lost at sea – accidents do happen!"

"Brilliant! That is brilliant," Esman said.

"Yes it is; if I may say so," Iltar reaffirmed; then said, "If I were to attend a meeting in Khun's office people would speculate; there is no reason for me to visit his office, on the other hand, you are our Chief Ambassador and meeting with the generals to discuss military treaties is one of your duties.

"So let's arrange a meeting with General Khun; in the palace; in your office.

"I will enter your office from the adjacent one. Make sure that your assistant is not in his office or the palace during the meeting."

"That won't be a problem," Esman said.

"Well...then arrange a meeting for tomorrow morning."

"Will do," Esman said; then left the room, went to his office, placed a call to General Khun's office and arranged the meeting; that done he called his assistant and assigned him a task that should keep him away all morning.

******

Next morning, General Khun – riding a chariot – was on his way to the Royal Palace located in the Central Island.

The Central Island could only be reached by boat using a subterranean water channel that led to the sea or by four bridges that converged at the Central Island from the four cardinal points of the compass. The roadway was wide enough to accommodate two chariots side by side.

General Khun was now at the outer wall of the third ring water belt; he was about to enter the first of the six gate-towers that he will encounter on his way to the Central Island.

The gate-towers were self-sufficient; provisioned with all that a military garrison would need; including living quarters for the guards, and stables for the horses and chariots used to patrol the walls of the islands.

Each tower had a gate that controlled the road traffic and another one that could be lowered to block off the water channel.

Khun crossed the first gate. On the other side; the causeway that led to the Race Course Island. He was now on his way heading for the bronze covered wall and gate-tower that protected the island. Once across the gate he had to go over a bridge that spanned the race track. There was one bridge on each one of the four roadways leading to the Central Island; this made possible to have a track surface without intersections. From this land bridge the general had a clear view of the buildings on the periphery of the race track: the Royal Grandstand, the Start-Finish Building, the Victors' Temple and the Military Barracks where most of Uranus' bodyguards were housed.

Going through another gate-tower Khun left the Race Course behind and – on the causeway – headed for the tin covered wall and gate-tower of the Grove of Poseidon Island.

Inside; an ethereal feeling pervaded the island. Small temples, fountains, and magnificent gardens covered the three-level island. Crossing another gate the general left the Grove of Poseidon Island behind.

Khun was now on the last causeway leading to the Central Island – the Acropolis; its wall and gate-tower were covered by a shiny metal – ORICHALC; an alloy of copper, aluminum, and platinum that would not tarnish or rust; it was found in its inherent state and as far as it was known the only existing mines were located in the Kingdom of Poseidia.

Once on the other side of the island access gate the general headed for the palace; before he reached it he went down a ramp on the right side of the roadway; it led to the palace basement where the stables were located.

Leaving the chariot in the basement Khun went up a long flight of stairs and came out in front of the palace; on the side that faced the Temple of Poseidon Plaza.

The Royal Palace had two wings connected by an arcade at the second floor level. The roadway that ended up at the Temple of Poseidon Plaza ran under this arcade.

Like all the palace offices, Ambassador Esman's office was on the first floor. On the second floor housing was provided for high officials and the palace staff. The Royal Apartments occupied the third floor. Uranus' quarters and the Throne Room were on the fourth floor.

Esman had been waiting for General Khun in his office and as soon as Khun entered the room Esman latched the front door and then opened the one that led to his assistant office where Iltar had been waiting.

Once they were seated it was Iltar who said, "General, we need your help so we can accomplish what we are planning. Nobody else must know; only the three of us. If we carry this out you will be rewarded with riches and a prestigious position."

"What do you have in mind?" the general asked.

Iltar answered, "I'm planning on taking over the throne when King Uranus dies; the way his health is deteriorating lately we think that it won't take long for that to happen."

"What about Chronus? He is the heir to the throne." the general questioned.

Iltar answered, "Chronus will die in an accident before the king dies. Being the High-Priest I will inherit the throne if there are no male heirs when the king dies."

Khun asked, "And how is that supposed to happen? I mean the accident."

Iltar answered, "That is where you come in. You must find the right person at the airfield; he must be willing to sabotage Chronus' vailx when he returns from Sais."

"Sabotage! That's a big word." Khun said.

"Yes, sabotage," Iltar said. "And it has to be done in such a way that if the ship is ever recovered it wouldn't be detected."

Esman added, "Pick a mechanic that services the military ships; one that doesn't work with the palace ships.

"Because of the backup mechanical and safety systems there had never been a fatal accident. Even if everything fails there are backup canopies that can be manually set free to bring the ship safely back to the ground.

"It wouldn't be hard to imagine what would happen to the mechanics that service Chronus' ship if it blows up in flight while he is flying it. Sabotage will be suspected and anybody that has anything to do with the ship will be submitted to brain scans. Every aspect of their in-and-out of the base personal interactions will also be looked at.

"General, that's why you must pick a mechanic that doesn't work on Chronus' ship. We don't want your name to come up if you had been seen talking to any of the mechanics that service the palace ships."

"Yes...I see," the general said.

Iltar asked, "Can we assume that a mechanic that services the military vailxi is familiar with the civilian ships?"

"He should be," the general answered. "Their propulsion and mechanical systems are identical. The difference is that the civilian ships are bigger, have luxurious interiors and are not equipped with military hardware – like weapons."

"Another thing," Iltar said. "Pick somebody that does not have a family."

"Why is that?" the general asked.

"Do you have a boat?" Iltar asked.

"Yes," the general responded. "But what does it has to do with all of this?"

"Well...we don't want any loose ends," Iltar answered. "As soon as the sabotage is done you must go sailing with the mechanic. It is important that whoever sees you with him will think that he is doing some maintenance work on your boat. Make sure that he doesn't make it back to shore with you – he fell overboard and was never seen again."

"Very clever," the general said.

"Do you have somebody in mind?" Iltar asked.

"Yes...I think that I have the perfect candidate," the general answered. "There is a widower, no family, about to retire, and if it is true what I heard about him I know that I can convince him. He spends most of his free time in the canteens raising hell, and most important he doesn't seem to have any savings for his retirement. I'm sure that he can be convinced if offered a large sum of silver currency."

"Well..., then get him," Iltar said.

"Most important," Esman added. "Tell him to sabotage the ship as soon as Chronus returns from Sais, even if you are not in Semira. You could be on a mission, like the one that we are planning to Mohenjo-Daro.

"As soon as he agrees to do it we would like to know his name – just in case."

"No problem," the general said.

"If we agree, then...let's do it," Iltar said as he headed for the adjacent office.

The meeting was over.

Khun went down to the palace basement; retrieved his chariot and rode it to the Large Ocean Port, then went over to the funicular station and on a passenger pod headed for his office at the air base.

When Khun reached his office he went straight to a file cabinet where the base personnel records were kept; removed the record folder of the mechanic that he had in mind; checking it over the general found out what he needed to know – as he thought before, the man seemed to be the perfect candidate.

The general returned the folder to the cabinet and then walked over to the military maintenance office; there he located the crew chief and asked him if he could talk to one of his mechanics; gave him the name, then to establish an alibi told the chief that he wanted to find out if this man, on his day off, was willing to work on his sailboat.

Khun waited in the office. The chief went to where the mechanic was working; found the man and returned with him to the office.

The general told the mechanic that he wanted to talk to him – outside. They left the office and walked toward one of the landing pads; out there Khun explained to the man what he wanted done and offered a very large sum of silver currency; enough to buy a farm and slave workers. The man agreed to do it.

Khun questioned the mechanic about what kind of malfunction could cause what they had in mind; and that it could not be detected before the flight or after the accident if parts of the ship were ever recovered.

Satisfied with the mechanic proposed scheme the general asked, "Are you sure that what you are proposing can be done without incriminating yourself?"

"Yes I do," the mechanic answered. "All I have to do is to hide in the parts storage room of the palace hangar just before they close the hangar doors – they do it at sundown.

"I'll have all night to work on the ship. Uranus' ship is assigned the number one pad and Chronus is assigned the number two pad.

"In the morning, if they see me in or around the parts room I wouldn't look out of place. It would look as if I was trying to locate and borrow a part that I needed; we do it all the time. They also borrow parts from our military parts room."

The general then said, "I want you to do it the first night after the ship is back. It doesn't matter if I'm not around. There are two high officials that will know your name. You will get paid – no matter what.

"Oh, and this is important; I told your crew chief that the reason that I wanted to talk to you was to see if you could do some work on my boat. If your co-workers are curious about why a general is talking to you; you know what to say."

With the pact consummated the general went back to his office.

CHAPTER 10

It was his last day of training. Torr will fly around the continent; his first long distance solo flight.

Waiting for Kalac – Torr wandered about the base; he was familiar with the work done by the priests that worked on the ships but because of his training schedule he had never seen what was being done in the labs; this seemed a good time to find out, a lab was right in front of him; a metallurgical lab; he entered the lab and after exchanging greetings with the priests asked, "What are you working on?"

The older of the two priests answered, "We are about to transmute liquid mercury into a solid metal – gold."

"Are you serious?" Torr questioned.

"Oh yes. It is a very simple operation, we do it all the time," the priest said.

"I was not aware that we use gold – it is not used for jewelry; so, what do we use it for?" Torr asked.

The priest replied, "Contacts and terminals in the electrical circuits are gold plated. Gold is an excellent conductor and will not rust. Only a small quantity is needed so it makes sense to transmute the mercury instead of extracting the gold from the ground, it's easier and we have plenty of mercury."

"Will you please explain how you do it?" Torr asked.

The priest told him, "You will learn all there is to know during your training. For now, we can give you an idea about the mechanics of how it is done. As you must know, there is hardly any difference between the mercury and gold atom nucleuses."

"Yes I know that." Torr said.

"Good!" the priest said. "Then, let me give you a simple explanation. If we take out the extra clump from the mercury atom nucleus the electron shells will rearrange their orbits to conform to the new nucleus configuration - the mercury atom becomes a gold atom.

"Understood?" the priest asked.

"Yes," Torr answered.

Torr then noticed on a table what appeared to be some crystal granules and asked, "What are those granules, are they used in the process?"

"Yes they are," the priest answered. "They are needed to transmute the mercury."

"How is that so?" Torr asked.

"Let me explain," the priest answered. "It has to do with the atomic structure of the crystal; its sulfur and zinc atoms serve a dual purpose.

"First, the crystal is piezoelectric – and we need to generate an electrical current inside the mercury atom.

"Second, the frequency of oscillation of the two atoms when submitted to high temperature and pressure can be modulated to replicate the frequency of the master-etheric-pattern that created the gold atoms.

"To accomplish this we introduce the mercury and the crystals in the sealed ball-shaped container, then using a frequency generator we oscillate the mercury; that increases the temperature and pressure inside the container.

"The increase in temperature vaporizes the mercury – a mist is created.

"The increase in pressure generates an electrical current due to the piezoelectric properties of the crystal; and that is what we need to dislodge a proton from the nucleus of each one of the mercury atoms in the misty cloud inside the container.

"The master-etheric-pattern created by the process transmutes the mercury mist into a solid piece of gold."

The priest had just finish saying that when somebody said, "There you are," it was Kalac; now standing at the shop door.

"I'm sorry," Torr said.

"I'm the one to blame," Kalac said, "I was late leaving my house; had to take care of a sick hound. Now, let's go to the control room – you need a flight plan."

Once in the control room Kalac spread a map of the Murovian Continent on a table and using a marker traced the route that he wanted Torr to follow; then he told him, "You have the rest of the day to do it. Time your speed so that you spend the rest of the day out there. Learn to recognize the topography of the continent; the location of the rivers, cities, villages, roads, and all the landmarks that could help you navigate if the guidance system malfunctions."

Kalac folded the map; gave it to Torr and said, "Now is up to you – time to stretch your wings! I want to talk to you when you get back."

"I'll do that," Torr said; then left the office.

Torr went directly to the ship; inspected its outer surfaces, went aboard, and after checking the status of all the systems started the mercury boiling cycle. When it reached the operational temperature and pressure he engaged the propulsion system and slowly lifted the ship off the ground; and then proceeded to guide it to the exit-entry tunnel. Once outside he flew eastward.

At a safe distance from the base he gained altitude and headed for Kupol the largest city and seaport on the Eastern side of the continent.

Torr had flown many times over Kupol during his flight training and was familiar with the area landmarks so there was no reason for him to linger over the region. The moment the ship overflew Kupol he started to follow the seashore – heading north.

The next large city was Trell; once over the city Torr was treated to a unique spectacle; the fishermen returning to port; their boats darting from side to side as they sailed to windward. The bay was full of white sails that danced against the backdrop of the dark blue sea. Torr circled the area a few times then resumed his heading.

Next town ahead, Rowen; where he had attended college the last seven years.

Once Torr reached Rowen he held the ship in position over the Temple College and with the magnifying screen took a look at his former school. The school yard was full of students, it was break time; soon they would go back to the classrooms.

Lifting his eyes from the screen he glanced toward the sea and saw them; the two small islands located just outside the Bay of Rowen; that's where the accident happened.

With a feeling of sadness he left the area and resumed his flight along the coast on his way to Liss, this time heading west. On the way there he flew over a large fishing village; Wont. After a cursory look at the area landmarks he continued on his flight.

Torr was born and lived for the first twelve years of his life on a small village not far from Liss so he knew his way around Liss.

He reached Liss; now over the bay; to his left Kalac's house, and to his right on the other side of the bay the Sailors' Temple.

Liss was Muror's larger city and the commercial hub of the empire; it had a population of about 1,000,000.

Slowly moving inland he overflew the docks where about a hundred ships were tied down; being loaded or unloaded – an impressive sight.

He reached the market square; it was still early and was full of merchants and their customers. At noon the merchants would collect their wares and with the customers leave the square.

Unlike the smaller cities and villages he had flown over there was a lot of vehicular traffic; hundreds of hound-carts were going up and down the streets.

Torr flew back to the coast, made a left turn and headed for Barb; Muror's boatbuilding center.

Like Liss, Barb was located on a very large bay; it wasn't that far away so it didn't take long to get there.

Flying over the city he saw the temple where he would be now had not fate intervened.

At the bay; the shipyards; a lot of ship skeletons were seen on dry land; eventually they will end up as river boats or seagoing ships.

Once Torr was sure that he could recognize the area landmarks he resumed flying in a western direction.

When he reached the westernmost region of the continent he changed his heading; this time heading south – toward Tuin; a vacation resort for the rich.

By the time Tuin materialized on the horizon it was noon already. So, Torr decided to take a lunch break; he stopped the forward motion of the ship and activated the ship automatic hovering-in-place mode.

All the ships were equipped for long range flights. A lavatory was located in a small cubicle behind the center column, and opposite the lavatory, below the rear facing windows a locker provided storage space for snacks, water, and the emergency equipment.

As Torr walked over to the food locker he realized that in the excitement of the moment – his first long range solo flight – he forgot to request that food be provided for the flight. Torr opened the locker and found his lunch; whoever put it there must have known he was going to be out all day.

He ate his lunch while the ship hovered in place, then took a peek at the map and resumed his flight.

As he approached Tuin he saw the lakes that the city was famous for; steam was rising from their surfaces. Tuin was famous for its mud baths and thermal waters.

Torr left Tuin behind and headed for the Ayas Province, for the city of Ober; a seaport; it was the largest and most important city of that province.

Once he overflew Ober Torr did some calculations and determined that to get back to the base before sundown he must fly faster. Adjusting his speed he continued flying around the continent, now at a higher speed.

******

Torr landed at the base on schedule.

As soon as he came out of the ship he was told that Kalac was waiting for him at Flight Operations; when he entered the office Kalac told him, "I see that you made it back – in one piece!"

Torr grinned approval; then said, "Yes, but it was a grueling flight due to all that zigzagging."

Kalac said, "Well...but you did it! That means that you are ready; ready to do the job that you were trained for.

"The Archpriest wants to talk to you before you go on your first mission; but before you do that I want you to take a few days off. Visit your parents; tell them that you have been reassigned to the Scribes' Temple.

"Your parents live in a small village near Liss; you can use one of my hound-carts to get there.

"Pack what you need for a few days and be ready to leave before dawn. I will pick you up in the morning – be at the hangar when I land."

Kalac then left the base and went home.

******

Next day Kalac was back before dawn; Torr was waiting for him. Torr went aboard; and with him at the controls they took off and disappeared into the night.

By the time they landed at Kalac's house the sun was beginning to rise over the Eastern horizon.

A hound-cart was already waiting by the front door – Torr then went on his way.

CHAPTER 11

Uranus was back; his pilot dropped him off on the palace roof late at night – nobody noticed.

******

The next morning the news that Uranus was back spread like wildfire.

As soon as Iltar heard the news he tried to secure an audience with the king but was informed that he will have to wait at least five days. It seems that there were other urgent matters with a higher priority.

A disappointed Iltar returned to his office; Esman was waiting for him.

"We have a problem," it was the first thing that Iltar heard from Esman when he entered his office.

"Now what?" Iltar asked.

"I mean a big problem," Esman explained. "General Khun contacted me. It seems that our man; the mechanic, has second thoughts about his safety after he sabotages Chronus' vailx. He wants an official military order, in writing; stating that he was ordered to do what he did. And of course, the general must sign the order in his presence. He plans on leaving the sealed document with a trusted friend; to be handed over to the authorities if he were to die under suspicious circumstances."

"Oh boy!" Iltar said. "The man is no fool."

Esman asked, "So, what are we going to do?"

"An interesting dilemma," Iltar answered. "We can't let somebody else, a stranger at that, get involved in our plot. Yet, we have to go ahead with the plan."

There was a long silence from both of the men, then all of a sudden Iltar said, "Yes...that's it."

"Have you found a solution?" Esman asked.

Iltar answered, "Do you remember when we were in school? In our science class; the teacher demonstrated how a certain acid released fumes that made the writing on a scroll disappear."

"Oh yes, I remember," Esman replied; then asked, "What do you have in mind?"

"Well...we can comply with what the man wants and at the same time be on the safe side." Iltar said.

"How are you planning on doing that?" Esman asked.

Iltar answered, "We need one of those canisters with a glass lining that we use to store important documents. All we have to do is modify the cap so that when you screw it all the way it will release the fumes."

"I see," Esman said; then asked, "But what is to prevent the man from opening it before he gives it to somebody for safekeeping?"

"Yes, that would be a problem," Iltar said. "This is what we'll do; with the mechanic present, the general will sign the scroll, insert it in the canister and screw the cap all the way; after all that is done he will seal the cap junction with the official hard wax seal of the empire in such a way that if somebody removes the cap it will break the seal. The general then will imprint the seal with the stamp used to safeguard the original copies of our important documents. As you know the stamp reads, 'For the contents to be considered authentic you must open the canister in the presence of a certified government official; otherwise the contents would be considered a forgery'. That for sure will deter them from opening it."

Esman said, "I would like to see the face of whoever opens the canister and finds a blank scroll."

"Yes, I imagine," Iltar said.

Esman asked, "How are we going to do it?"

Iltar said, "Let's go down to the basement storehouse and get one of the canisters with an internal glass lining."

They went down to the basement, found what they were looking for and returned to the office to figure out how to modify the cap.

After many attempts they found a solution. Iltar took some measurements, made some drawings; gave them to Esman and told him, "Have each part done by a different shop; that way it will be impossible for somebody to figure out what they are for. Once we get the parts it is up to us to assemble the device. Offer to pay extra if they can deliver the part by tomorrow afternoon."

As Esman was leaving Iltar told him, "By the way, I almost forgot to tell you that I must wait at least five days before I can get an audience with Uranus."

"Well...I will be..." Esman was heard mumbling as he left the office,

******

In two days the canister was ready and loaded with acid; once that was done Iltar told Esman, "Now go and give it to the general; make sure he understands what we want done and how to do it so that the mechanic wouldn't suspect anything."

Esman went to the palace basement and requested the use of a chariot; it was much faster than waiting for a boat.

At the base Esman found Khun in his office, took the canister out of a canvas satchel and placed it over his desk, then told him what they were planning on doing. After making sure that everything was understood Esman handed over the canister, stood up and told the general that he was going back to his office at the palace.

******

Next day the mechanic was summoned to Khun's office.

The scroll and the canister were over the table.

The general handed the scroll to the man; he read it.

Khun then asked, "Are you satisfied?"

"Yes, it looks acceptable to me."

The general affixed his signature, inserted the scroll in the canister; closed it and applied the seal and then went on to explain what the seal was for and its importance.

Once Khun was sure that the man understood what breaking the seal implicated he handed it over.

The mechanic left the office with a grin on his face thinking that he had outwitted the ones behind the plot – little did he knew.

CHAPTER 12

Three days had gone by. Torr was back and at the controls of Kalac's airship as they overflew Liss on their way to Nalta.

As they flew over Liss Kalac suggested, "Let's follow the river so that you can acquaint yourself with the relevant landmarks of both sides of the river."

Torr proceeded to head for the river and started to follow its course. Once they left Liss behind he saw the village, the village of Kabor where he was born and where he had been the last three days. He stopped the ship forward motion and told Kalac, "There, to your left; Kabor, where my parents live."

Kalac then said, "Since we are so close let's take a look. Use the magnifying screen and try to locate your parents' house."

Torr held the ship in position over the village.

The house was easy to locate; they took a look at it and at the rest of the village. Having seen all there was to see Kalac said, "Go back and continue flying over the river."

Torr resumed his flight.

******

When they reached the Nalta canal junction Torr changed course and continued flying over the canal. To the left of the canal; the Ayas Province, and to his right the mud fields where the Phara pottery industry was located.

They overflew Nalta and came in from the west. The temple was located on the western side of the city. Torr was now over the lake and started his approach to the waterfall. Realizing that it was impossible to see where the tunnel was Torr stopped the ship forward motion, looked at Kalac and asked, "Now what? How can I tell where the tunnel is?"

"I was about to tell you," Kalac said; then he slid his hand under the control panel, unblocked a lever, flipped it and explained, "This lever tells the automatic guidance system to locate the four probes that delimit the tunnel opening; then it will guide you in; hands-off."

"So, that's what it is for" Torr said; adding, "I noticed the lever during my preflight checks but since I was never told what it was for during my flight training I assumed that – being blocked – it must have something to do with the servicing of the ship. How come I wasn't told?"

Kalac answered, "There was no need for you to know while you were training. This is the only place where you will ever need to use that lever. Now, go ahead and take us in and park the ship."

Torr let the guidance system take over; once on the other side of the waterfall he disengaged it and guided the ship to the cavern underneath the Great Temple.

The gatekeeper escorted the visitors to the Archpriest private meeting room. The Archpriest was waiting for them and when they entered the room he said, "Welcome...please be seated," then looking at Torr said, "If you are here it means that you are ready."

"Ready as can be," Torr said.

"Yes, we are sure of that," the Archpriest said. "There are some rules and other facts that you should be familiar with so that you can safeguard your identity – here and during your missions.

"People, in this country and elsewhere, are under the impression that we only have three airships; the ones used to transport our ambassadors, dignitaries, and members of my household. It is common knowledge that two of the ships are stationed here and that the other one is at Kalac's home. The only places where those ships are seen landing are: here at the temple, Kalac's home, and at the scribes' village – Tabchi. The ships can land in public places if flown by my pilots or Kalac; that applies here in Muror and in foreign lands.

"During undercover missions you must hide your ship when you land in foreign countries. If for some reason you are flying the repulsion drive ship do not land. There is one exception – our secret outpost.

"You have finished your initial training and can move to the house in the village, when you get back from this trip Kalac will drop you off at the village so that you can select the furnishings for your house. If we need you one of my pilots or Kalac will pick you up at the village landing pad. The villagers and their priest will be told that at times I may need your services as a scribe. If your future missions last more than one day you will stay at the base, the villagers will assume that you are here at the temple."

The Archpriest had just finished saying that when a woman dressed in a white tunic entered the room – it was the Arch Priestess; unlike in her public appearances when she wore a lot of jewelry, the only adornments she was wearing were a silver belt wrapped around her waist and a pair of silver bracelets.

"Good day to all," she said; and then looking at Torr, "I heard a lot of good things about you. I'm told that you are leaving on your first mission and I have never seen you. I came over to see what you look like – so that I will be able to recognize you."

The Archpriest added, "Yes...like me, she has to be able to recognize all of our Priest-Scientists; that's why we visit the base once a year."

The Arch Priestess then said, "Please go ahead with whatever you are doing."

The Archpriest continued, "Now...what we are going to tell you is a guarded secret – in Muror only seven of us know of its location or that it exists; you will be the eight. As you already know 14,000 years ago the polar shift broke apart the continent of Atlantis and divided it into five big islands.

"Well...we took advantage of the rebuilding chaos and were able to build a secret outpost in an isolated region of Poseidia. Beside the four, here present, there are only four others that know about the outpost, they are: Caleb; his assistant, and my two pilots. There is also a priest and a priestess at the outpost; Kalac will show you its location.

"If you get married you can't tell your wife or any of your children about the existence of the outpost. Are there any concerns that you may want to talk about? Any doubts?"

Torr answered, "No, everything is understood and I'm eager to carry out my duties."

The Archpriest then asked Kalac, "When can he be on his way?"

Kalac answered, "Tomorrow if we get back to the base today. I have to brief him and we have to get his ship ready."

"Good, that is good," the Archpriest said. "You may go now. The Gods be with you," then he stood up and left the room with the Arch Priestess.

Kalac and Torr went down to the hangar. As they walked over to the ship Torr took a quick look toward the tunnel and saw a gate of metal bars at the entrance of the tunnel, so he asked, "Where did that gate came from? I didn't see it before, and I have been here two times.

Kalac answered, "The first time that you flew out of here you didn't look that way when you entered the hangar, you were looking at the ships.

"Whenever we start the engine of any of the ships here in the hangar a signal is transmitted to open the gate – it is automatic. When we came in from the outside the probes at the entrance activated the mechanism and by the time you get to where the gate is it is already open. There is a time delay after the engine is shut down, that's the reason you didn't notice when we came in – by the time the gate closed we were in our way to the meeting room."

"Well, well...impressive," Torr said.

Once aboard Torr started the engine and glanced toward the gate; it was moving, opening.

As soon as the ship emerged on the other side of the waterfall Kalac said, "Slow down, I want to show you how the waterfall is created and its purpose. Take a look down there, water is pumped from the lake into the pool that feeds the waterfall. As for the waterfall purpose; the angle of the water flow on the waterfall sides sucks stale air from the cavern.

"The landing pad that you see near the temple is used by visiting ships."

"Yes I see it," Torr said. "I didn't notice it before because we left in a hurry when we were flown to your home by the Archpriest pilot, and today my attention was focused on the lake and the waterfall."

"Now...head for the base," Kalac ordered.

Torr complied with the order.

******

Once they reached the base they went directly to flight operations; borrowed some maps and joined Caleb who was waiting for them in his office. They spread the maps of Poseidia over the table; Kalac selected the one where the secret outpost was located and then told Torr, "There is one place in Atlantis that eventually you will have to visit; their capital; Semira; and there is no safe place to land and hide the ship at a reasonable distance.

"Our secret outpost is the only safe place to land that is close enough to Semira; it is not shown in any of our maps so we'll show you how to get there. Do you remember when we flew over the Granite Mountains and I told you to take a good look? Well, that's where it is located."

"Yes I remember," Torr said.

"Then," Kalac said. "I will explain how to approach the outpost and how to land there.

"You must always start your approach about a hundred miles out and fly close to the surface of the sea; this must be done just before dawn. Locate the gorge created by the two tallest peaks; fly toward the gorge, at the shoreline you will see a stream; follow it, eventually you will encounter a granite mountain with a very steep slope, stop and climb until you see a narrow ledge on the vertical face of the mountain, stop.

"Scan the skies; make sure that there are no other ships in sight, then, follow the same routine as when you land here at the base. It is an automated system; if it recognizes your identification code it will open the door.

"The door will close as soon as sensors detect that the ship is inside and resting on the ground.

"Once the door closes you will find yourself in total darkness. Use the ship internal lights while waiting.

"The opening of the door generates a flashing light at the priest house; he then goes over and opens the secret door that leads to the tunnel and his house.

"Write down the coordinates of the two mountains so that the automatic guidance system will take you there. Remember that you must approach the mountains before the sun rises over the horizon – that means night flying."

Torr made a sketch of the terrain and wrote down the approach coordinates.

Caleb then said, "I suggest that you memorize the sketch and then destroy it; we don't want it to fall in the wrong hands, even if they are friendly hands."

The briefing was over so Kalac said, "Now you know about our secret outpost. Eventually, to carry out your mission you will have to land at the outpost.

"But first, you have to contact Queen Moo; and as far as we know she was last seen on a boat heading for Sais.

"So, let's go back to the hangar. We have to get your ship ready for your trip to Sais."

They folded the maps and returned them to the flight controller's office, and then they went back to the ship to make sure that the survival gear was on-board.

Torr will require a special wardrobe to carry out his covert operations. Diverse outfits of the world clothing styles were available at the base foreign wardrobe locker; and that's where they went first.

The first disguise selected was a sailor's outfit. All sailors, no matter from what country, wear the same basic type of clothing; a short tunic. The Atlanteans urban outfits; that was a different story; it consisted of pants, jackets and boots instead of the tunics used in Muror. Clothing to conform to the different styles used by the countries that Torr may have to visit was selected. And last but not least important, coins from all regions of the world were also selected.

They loaded the items on the ship and checked that the inflatable boat was in working order.

The only thing left to do was to order that water and food is loaded next morning; and it was done.

There was nothing else to do but wait for tomorrow.

******

Next morning Torr spent a few hours checking the ship and making sure that everything that he may need was aboard; then he waited. He was eager to go but there was nothing he could do but wait. He must depart just before noon; otherwise he would have to wait many hours in the dark before he could cross the swamp.

Kalac showed up and they talked about the mission, and about his new home in the village.

Finally it was time to leave. Once aboard the ship Torr started the engine, lifted-off, entered the entry-exit tunnel and left the base behind.

As the ship raced toward darkness he questioned if he could endure the demands that fate had imposed on him - a life of solitude.

Torr followed the same route that he had flown with Kalac; this time at a lower altitude.

The ship gained on the sun; overtook it and arrived at the delta just before first light. Torr activated the beacon; positioned the ship over it and started his descent. Just as he was about to land the glimmering rays of the sun appeared over the horizon announcing a new day.

After landing Torr removed the inflatable boat and the camouflage net from their compartment; covered the ship with the net so that it couldn't be seen from the air, then, after changing his appearance to look like an Atlantean sailor took the boat out and inflated it.

Crossing the swamp was harder than what he had figured out, he had to cut a lot of vines to get through.

He reached the seashore, found a place to hide the boat and started walking toward the boat terminal; once there he joined some sailors that were waiting for the boat that would take them to Sais.

It was mid-morning when the boat showed up; everybody went aboard and the boat sailed upriver. Unlike the Murovian River boats this one was sail powered.

As they went along Torr corroborated what they had seen when they flew over this area. There were marshes on one side and high ground on the other side. The high ground was about thirty feet above the river water level. Sais was on the high side – to their left as they sailed upriver.

******

It was almost midnight by the time they arrived at Sais. Torr needed a place to stay that night. The sailors seemed to know their way around so Torr followed them and ended up at a sailors' inn where he rented a room.

******

Up at first light Torr was out exploring the city; he saw a man carrying a bale; probably a farmer on his way to the market. He asked the man, "Good man, do you know if Queen Moo is here in Sais?"

The man answered, "I believe that she left Sais, if that is so you better inquire at the boat terminal, they should know if she did leave and where she headed for."

After thanking the man Torr walked over to the boat terminal.

There was a lot of activity at the dock. A lot of carts full of goods were waiting to be shipped out and empty carts were ready to receive the incoming goods.

The first boat agent that Torr talked to referred him to the one that had to do with the boat that Queen Moo sailed on.

The agent confirmed that the queen did sail in one of his boats and that her final destination was the Maioo Colony, a Naga settlement.

Torr didn't want to waste another day. He must find a way to reach the Maioo Colony that same day before sundown. There has to be enough daylight so that he can find a suitable spot to land and hide the ship; but, for that to be possible he has to be back to the ship in about eight hours and he was beginning to believe that it was not possible. Then, he remembered the chariots that ran parallel to the river.

Maybe there was a chance, he thought. The cart rental agency was located by the boat terminal. He saw the stables and walked over, found the agent and asked, "Can you get me to the Inland Sea in four hours if we leave right now?"

The agent thought it over and said, "Well...that may be possible, but, it will cost you plenty. The driver will have to stop at eight relay stations to get a fresh team. If the chariot runs at maximum speed it might be possible, it will be close and may take more time – at the most another half-an-hour."

After haggling over the price Torr accepted, and wasting no time they were on their way. The driver demanded from the animals their maximum effort and the chariot seemed to swallow the road – it was a bone rattling ride.

After enduring the pounding for four-and-a-half hours Torr made it back to the river end; he was glad that the torture was over.

Still shaken and sore from the ride he started walking, he must get back to where the inflatable boat was hidden so he turned his beacon locator on. Once he found the boat he inflated it and started paddling. The return trip was easier; there were no vines to cut.

******

Torr made it back to the ship on schedule, and after storing the net and the boat, took-off and headed for the Maioo Colony – a small Naga colonial settlement on the Red Sea straits.

At maximum speed it didn't take long to reach his destination.

Farming was being done on the flat lands that ran parallel to the seashore. Inland – to the west – there were some small hills that appeared to be uninhabited, and most important there were a lot of trees and bushes, a good place to hide the ship.

Torr used the magnifying screen to check the wooded hills – looking for a safe place to land. No trails or signs of human activities were discernible in the area. He found what appeared to be a good place to land; it was close enough to the settlement.

Torr fired a homing beacon into the ground, then took the ship to a higher altitude and waited for darkness; after a short wait he landed and camouflaged the ship. Now, he must wait for daylight.

******

In the morning as soon as the sun illuminated the sky Torr headed for the settlement dressed as a sailor wearing a short tunic.

It took two hours to reach the settlement; once there Torr went straight to the docks; there he asked a sailor, "Is it true that the Queen of Mayax is here?"

"She is," the man answered, "but I heard that she is leaving tomorrow."

"Do you know where she is heading for?" Torr asked.

"It is known that she secured passage for Sais; from there we heard that she is heading back home to Mayax."

Torr asked, "Do you know where she is staying?"

"At the High-Priest home," the man said.

"I thank-you." Torr told the man.

After hearing the news Torr concluded that it would be impossible to approach the queen before her departure if he wanted to keep his identity a secret. If he had more time; a few days, it would be possible to find out about her daily routine and figure out a way to contact her in private; evidently that was not possible. Torr would have to contact her while she was on her way to Sais.

Torr located the boat agent; told him that he was thinking on going to Sais and would like to know on how to get there.

The agent told Torr, "It will take five days to reach the seaport terminal where you must stay overnight. Next day you will transfer to the overland trail. After four days and four relay stations you will end up at the delta station. The next morning a river boat will take you downriver all the way to Sais. Well...there you have it."

That's all Torr needed to know. If he can't make contact before her departure his next opportunity would be at the seaport terminal inn where the passengers must stay overnight; it should be easy for him to approach her there.

The rest of the day Torr tried to find a way to contact Queen Moo but as he suspected it was not possible, she never left the priest home.

Torr stayed that night at a sailors' inn.

******

Before dawn Torr was up and watching the loading of the boat. The passengers arrived after they finished loading the cargo.

Queen Moo and her maids were now going aboard. In any case he did get to see what the queen looked like.

It was time to get back to his ship – he has a plan on how to approach her at the terminal inn.

******

Torr was back at the ship in three hours; removed the net, took-off and started flying north looking for the seaport terminal; once he found it he started flying on a spiral pattern looking for a suitable place to land; found it not far from the terminal and shot a homing beacon into the ground.

The spot was now ready for a night landing. He will return in five days.

After marking the spot Torr headed for the base; once at high altitude he advised them of his return by sending the usual coded message – returning to base.

******

When Torr landed Kalac was waiting for him; then, they headed for Caleb's office – to debrief Torr.

Kalac was the first to ask, "Well...what did you learn? What is happening?"

Torr answered, "I found the queen but was unable to contact her; she left the Maioo Colony the day after I arrived. She is on her way back to Sais and I plan to contact her when she stops for the night at the Red Sea Seaport Terminal."

"We want to hear what you have in mind," Caleb said.

Torr told them about his plan. The plan: Torr will be at the inn when the queen arrives and he will hand a locket to her while she is being escorted to her room.

As for the locket; On the outside face of a small locket; the Muror Empire seal, and the inscription 'Do not open in the presence of others' – inside; 'The bearer is an Archpriest of Muror envoy, please arrange a private meeting with him'.

They approved the plan. All there was to do was to wait...

CHAPTER 13

Iltar finally did get his audience with Uranus. He was now in front of the throne room door waiting to be shown in. The usher opened the door and announced him. Iltar entered the room and as always was overwhelmed by its opulence. The throne; made of solid gold and embellished with precious stones. The columns and floor were of white marble with blue speckles. Light blue walls and ceiling with gold trim.

As Iltar approached the throne Uranus said, "Iltar, old friend, what are you up to now? They tell me that you have a crazy proposal for me. What is it? Now...now, tell me."

"Your Excellency, if I may say so, it is not as crazy as you may have heard. What we propose will increase the treasury revenues and at the same time could provide some needed first hand combat experience for our assault forces and pilots."

Uranus asked, "What do you mean by 'we'? And how would that scheme of yours work?"

"Your Excellency, this plan was conceived by three of us; General Khun, General Darko, and myself.

"We are planning on offering Military Protection Treaties to the Naga Empire. There are a lot of barbaric tribes on their Western frontier and eventually Naga Provinces will be attacked.

"The treaties will generate extra income. Also, we may be able to secure some other trade agreements in the region.

"Your Excellency, as you can see, it's a win-win situation. Extra income for our treasury and live target practice for our vailx pilots if we ever have to defend them from the nomad tribes."

Uranus thought about it for a moment and after mumbling some unintelligible words said, "Hmm...Well, if you think that it is a good idea, go ahead, do it."

"A wise decision Your Excellency."

"Now go," Uranus told Iltar. "There are other problems that need my attention."

Iltar left the room with a grin on his face. The old man was not what he used to be; he didn't challenge the proposal like he used to do.

Now he must hurry and contact Esman. Generals Darko and Khun must be told that they have Uranus approval and to proceed as planned.

Iltar went over to Esman office and gave him the news.

"At last!" Esman exclaimed; then asked, "Did you call the generals?"

"No, that would be too risky," Iltar said. "You better go over and tell them to proceed with the operation. Go now, get General Darko; go with him to the base and tell Khun, then hold a meeting with the officers. I want them to be on their way in four days."

Esman left his office, went to the palace basement and borrowed a chariot; headed for the Large Port, found General Darko in his office, and then accompanied him to the air base to brief the other officers.

At the base, they informed Khun that they have the approval, to proceed with the operation. Then, they had a meeting with the six officers to review their assignments; all of them agreed that the expected deadline could be met; take-off at dawn in four days.

As soon as the meeting broke off Esman returned to the palace and reported the outcome of the meeting to Iltar, then went to his office and placed a call to the ambassador that was going on the trip.

It didn't take long for the ambassador to show up; his office was close by.

After exchanging greetings Esman told him, "Sit down, I have to brief you on your next mission. You are leaving in four days."

"Four days!" the man exclaimed, surprised of such a short notice.

"Yes, four days," Esman repeated; then said, "You already know what has to be done, but this time there is going to be an alternate plan on how to proceed if the ruling priest refuses to go along with our proposal. We are planning on his demise if he doesn't accept our offer.

"Our ships will arrive at dawn so you will have all day to mingle with the priests and form an opinion as to which one will accept our terms; there is always a power-hungry one in each group. What you will be looking for is the candidate to replace the Rishi-King; if needed be.

"Try to approach them when they are alone, not in a group; that way you will be able to judge which one will do anything in his power to be elevated to the top position."

They talked some more about the mission and when the ambassador was ready to leave the office Esman reminded him that on the day of departure he must be at the base well before dawn.

CHAPTER 14

Queen Moo will arrive at the gulf seaport tomorrow; just before sunset; Torr has to be there before dawn the same day so that he can land the ship while darkness prevailed; the spot he had selected wasn't that far from the terminal, he has to be careful not to be seen while landing.

At the predetermined time Torr left the base and flew west following the same route he had flown before, crossed the day-night dateline and reached his target on time.

Once over the landing spot he had selected he activated the beacon, landed, covered the ship, and waited for the sun to create a new dawn.

At first light, carrying a small bag and dressed as a prosperous merchant he left the ship and walked over to the terminal inn; there he rented a room. Now all there was to do was to wait.

******

Late in the afternoon Torr went over to the docks and waited for the ship to materialize over the horizon.

Just before darkness covered the land he saw a speck appear over the horizon – it was a ship. Once the ship was close enough and he was sure that it was the right one he returned to the inn; there he waited at the end of the corridor that led to the dormitories. The queen must use that corridor to reach her room.

When the queen and her maids entered the corridor Torr walked toward her and just as she went by his side he dropped the locket. The queen stopped walking when she heard something hitting the floor.

Torr recovered the locket and told the queen, "You dropped this," and then handed it to her; face up.

Queen Moo looked it over, recognized the Muror seal and read the inscription on its face and was about to say something when Torr interrupted her.

Torr said, "It fell from your pocket."

Queen Moo took a good look at Torr, put the locket in her pocket and continued on her way. Once in her room she opened the locket to see what was inside. There was a written message and it seemed authentic; a symbol stamped at the end of the message meant that it came from the Archpriest of Muror. Only a few knew about its meaning, it was used during the exchange of confidential information between their two countries. She must find a way to talk to the envoy – in private.

During her trips the queen always had her meals in her room – and so her maids. This time she would send her maids to eat in the inn dining room; that would give the envoy a chance to contact her.

The queen told the maids, "Tonight I don't feel like having company while I eat my dinner. All of you can go down to the dining room and eat there. Tell the innkeeper that I want room service." then she told them what she wanted to have for dinner.

The maids went down to the dining room, told the innkeeper what the queen had requested, and that they will have their dinner in the inn dining room.

Torr had been waiting in the dining room and overheard what the maids told the innkeeper. It would take some time to prepare what the queen ordered; time enough for Torr to talk to the queen in private, so he went over to her room and knocked on her door.

Her maids were not present so the queen had to open the door; she saw that it was the man that gave her the locket so she said, "Come in young man."

Once Torr was in the room the queen closed the door and asked, "Now, tell me, who are you and why are you here? Why all the secrecy?"

Torr answered, "My name is Torr, and the reason that I'm here; it has come to the attention of the Archpriest of Muror that you are having problems with the Atlanteans and we would like to help; if that is possible. As for the secrecy; I'm sure you don't want your maids present for if you have a problem, I'm the one assigned to investigate and my identity must be kept a secret.

"Now, how about telling me what your problem is."

The queen said, "We have a Military Protection Treaty with the Poseidia Military Forces. Recently, an ambassador from Poseidia-Semira showed up in our kingdom; they are demanding some extra compensation not called for in the protection treaty; the payments not to be reported as part of the official treaty; and to be deducted from our exports to Poseidia."

Torr asked, "Do you know or have an idea of who is behind all this?"

"I have no idea, the ambassador only said that the extra payments were for some higher-ups; they promise that this will assure a faster response time if we ever need their help.

"My brother convinced me that we have no alternative, that we are powerless, and that if we don't accept the new demands they may kill us and subjugate our kingdom. I was so mad that I left him in charge and went to Sais; we knew that Chronus was there; it was my intention to find out if he has anything to do with the treaties but I found out that he doesn't. When I questioned him about the treaties he told me that after

Uranus approval it is up to the military and the ambassadors to negotiate the treaties.

"Their ambassador mentioned higher-ups; he didn't say Uranus or Chronus; so, we can assume that they are not aware of what is taking place.

"It is reasonable to surmise that the Chief Diplomat is implicated; it is improbable that one of his ambassadors will show up in a foreign land without his consent. As for the military; they need a general to carry out what was promised; but which one of them? That is for us to find out.

"There is a rumor that Uranus' mind is failing and that he is delegating most of his decision-making powers to the High-Priest and the military; this will tempt a power-hungry priest. If Chronus were to die and there is no heir to the throne when Uranus dies the High-Priest will inherit the throne. If I was Chronus I would watch my back.

"I didn't tell Chronus about what is happening because if they interrogate the ambassador they may never find out who his co-conspirators are. It is well known that the ambassadors are trained to resist brain scans and torture. I intended to see if I could find out how many are involved in the extortion plot before we tell Uranus.

"Their ambassador arrived in a military vailx and left the same way, the same day."

That was all Torr needed to know, so he told the queen, "I tell you what, we'll investigate and see what we can do. One of our ambassadors will inform you of the outcome of our intervention. Are you going back home?"

"Yes," the queen answered. "Back to Zahia our capital."

"Good," Torr said. "When you get back home act as if nothing happened. And another thing, if we ever coincide on any event or place you don't know me; we never met."

"Yes...of course," the queen said.

"I must leave now before your maids return," Torr said; then left the room, checked out of the inn and started walking toward where the ship was.

A crescent moon illuminated the road. After walking for about two hours Torr activated the homing beacon, then left the road and headed for the ship; found the ship, took-off and flew eastward.

******

It was near noon when he reached the base, landed, secured the ship and went straight to his dormitory; he hadn't slept for quite some time.

A message was transmitted to Kalac that Torr was back and that he would be resting for the rest of the day.

CHAPTER 15

Next morning, when Kalac landed Torr was already waiting for him. The first thing that Kalac asked Torr was, "How did it go? Were you able to make contact?"

"Yes," Torr answered.

"Then," Kalac said. "Let's go to Caleb's office so that you can tell us what is going on."

They went up the long flight of stairs that led to the Base Operations Office; there Kalac asked the priest in charge, "Is Caleb in his office?"

"Yes he is, and he is waiting for the two of you. I informed him when you landed. So go ahead."

Kalac knocked on the door, and then they went in.

When they entered the office Caleb stood up and said, "Welcome, please be seated."

Caleb's desk was an extra-large table suitable for examining large navigational charts.

Once they were seated Caleb asked Torr, "Now, tell us; what have you learned so far?"

Torr told them, "I was able to contact Queen Moo as planned – at the seaport terminal.

"It seems that some higher-ups from Poseidia-Atlantis are implicated in an extortion scheme."

"What do you mean?" Kalac asked.

"As it is known," Torr said, "Mayax has a Military Protection Treaty with Semira-Poseidia.

"According to the queen a Poseidia ambassador showed up at Mayax and informed them that from now on some higher-ups will retain an extra portion of the Mayax export proceeds; these extra payments not to be reported as part of the official treaty payments.

"The queen told me that it is likely that the Chief Ambassador is implicated in the plot because an ambassador was used; but that has to be proven because the ambassador arrived in a military ship, not in a palace ship as it would be if it was an official diplomatic visit.

"It is a safe bet that the military must be implicated because they used a military ship.

"The ambassador stayed there only one day, so there is no definite proof – yet – that the Chief Ambassador may know what is going on. An ambassador could be absent from his office for one day and it wouldn't raise any concerns; people may think that he was sick that day."

"What about Uranus and Chronus?" Kalac asked.

"Queen Moo believes that they are not aware of what is happening," Torr said. "The ambassador mentioned higher-ups; there was no mention of Uranus or Chronus."

After listening to all that Torr had to say about his meeting with the queen and discussing all the possible reasons behind what was going on, it was Kalac who said, "Torr has to go to Semira, we have to identify the ones implicated in the extortion plot; and then, we can take the necessary actions.

"Before Torr goes to Semira I have to inform the Archpriest of what the Atlanteans are up to," then looking at Torr said, "I'll drop you off at the village and pick you up this afternoon on my way back from Nalta.

"Your new house is ready. While at the village go to the local store and select the furnishings for the house; pick whatever is needed. The village priest will be of some help in determining what you need."

Caleb added, "There is a possibility that you may see my wife at the village, she took the day off from work. She knows who you are and you know her."

"Do I know her?" Torr asked.

"Yes you do know her, you met her when you visited the scribes; she is the Head Priestess in charge."

"I wasn't told that she was your wife." Torr said.

Caleb went on, "Today our daughter is coming back home from college; she graduated as a healer and will assist the present village healer, and become the village healer in a few months when he retires."

"Kalac then told Torr, "Well...let's go, there is much to be done today. I'll drop you off at the village."

They wasted no time leaving the base.

Torr was dropped off at the landing pad. The village priest showed up and both of them went over to the new house to determine what was needed. After taking a look at the interior of the house they headed for the store; once there Torr selected what was needed to furnish the house and was told that they would deliver the goods in two hours.

The village priest then suggested to Torr that while they waited for the furnishings to be delivered they could visit the village stores so that he would be familiar with what was available in each one of them.

After spending about an hour visiting the stores the priest said, "Let's go to the boat dock, it's about time for the boat arrival. Every ten days a boat brings the supplies that we don't produce locally; like the materials used by the scribes."

Torr remembered that Caleb's daughter was arriving that day so he asked, "Do they also transport passengers?"

"Oh yes, of course," the priest answered.

They went over to the boat dock; arriving just in time to see a boat coming their way.

As the boat came closer Torr noticed a few passengers on deck; only one was a woman; it must be Caleb's daughter, he thought.

The boat docked and the passengers disembarked. The woman seemed to be looking for somebody that was supposed to meet her. She noticed Torr; their eyes met and she smiled at him; his heart skipped a beat, her sparkling eyes reminded him of the woman that had to die so that he could fulfill his destiny.

Finally, a woman approached the young woman; Torr recognized her, it was Caleb's wife.

The two women hug each other and while doing so Caleb's wife noticed Torr and the village priest; then she and her daughter walked over to where Torr and the priest stood.

Caleb's wife seemed surprised to see Torr and asked him, "What are you doing here? Are you leaving on this boat?

Torr answered, "The priest is showing me around while I wait for the furnishings of my house to be delivered. Kalac will pick me up at the end of the day."

Caleb's wife said, "I didn't tell you my name when I first met you, my name is Omiga and this is Lena, my daughter. Lena, this is Torr; soon he will start working with us as a scribe."

"It's a pleasure meeting you," Lena said.

"Likewise," Torr said; then asked, "Can we help you with your bags?"

"Yes...of course...great," Lena said as she smiled at Torr; his heart skipped a beat again.

The priest and Torr carried her bags.

When they reached Caleb's house Omiga told Torr, "We would like you to come over for dinner the day that you start living in your new house."

"An offer that I gladly accept," Torr said. "On my first day, among other things, I have to find and contract a servant – I hope a good cook."

"That wouldn't be a problem," Omiga said. "We can help you select a good one from our labor pool."

"I'd appreciate that," Torr said.

Then Torr and the priest took their leave and headed for Torr's new house that was close by.

All of the 'scribes' homes were located in the same neighborhood; close to the temple.

The furnishings were delivered a short time after Torr and the priest arrived at the house.

The village priest helped Torr to unpack everything. It took three hours to arrange the furnishings, and to make sure that the kitchen appliances and the light torches were functional, and then, they headed for the landing pad.

Kalac must be about to return to pick up Torr.

While they walked toward the landing pad Torr asked, "Is Lena married or going to be married?"

"I was asking myself when you were going to ask, I saw how you looked at her, and how she looked at you," the priest said; then added, "No, she is not married or going to be married, it seems that the man, a school fellow, changed his mind when he found out that she wanted to live and work here where she grew up. He refused to live in an out of the way village."

At the landing pad they talked about the village life, and of course, Torr wanted to know more about Lena, so he asked, "Was Lena born here in Tabchi?"

"Yes, she was born here in Tabchi, I still remember, like if it was yesterday, how she used to spend most of her free time at the healer's clinic; always questioning what the healer was doing. She probably never imagined that one day she would be in charge of the clinic and that she would be a healer herself."

The priest had just finished talking when Kalac's ship materialized over the horizon. Kalac landed, and with Torr aboard took off.

Once airborne Kalac told Torr, "The Archpriest has given the go ahead, in three days you will be leaving for the Poseidia outpost, the priest will be expecting you.

"The next two days I want you to study the maps of Poseidia and memorize all the possible access routes from Semira to our outpost for you will have to return to the outpost by yourself.

"Also, check the Semira city maps; make sure that you know the location of their ports, the air base, and how to access the palace.

"The priest will take you to Semira and accompany you the first two days; enough time to acquaint you with the city layout and transport system. From then on you will be on your own, the priest will return to the outpost.

"I'll be back before you leave and brief you on what to look for."

"That would be a great help," Torr said.

Kalac dropped-off Torr at the base, and then flew back home.

That night, Torr couldn't get Lena out of his mind; perhaps, this was what God had in mind for him.

CHAPTER 16

For the last three days the Poseidia Air Assault Forces had been getting ready.

On the fourth day Esman showed up about an hour before departure time; he reviewed the mission objectives with the ambassador and afterward headed for the transports where Khun was making sure that everything needed was on-board. Esman asked Khun if he had informed the mechanic that he would be going on a mission and for him to be on the lookout for Chronus' ship; the general answered that he had done so.

The only things left to be loaded; the vailxi fighters; they were now hovering behind the transports; two of them behind each ship.

As the vailxi moved forward they were latched to the retractable beams.

With the vailxi loaded the ready lights were activated in the transports, and the stand by lights came on.

Not long after they finished loading the fighters the Eastern horizon heralded a new dawn; a shining arc of light became visible over the mountain peaks.

It was time to go. The two egg-shaped ships took to the air and after rising above the mountain peaks headed for Lixus; their first checkpoint on the seventeen hour trip.

******

Eight hours later, on their way to the second checkpoint, daylight gradually faded and the sinister shadows of darkness took over. The Inland Sea was no longer visible; from then on the stars would guide them.

******

An hour before the estimated time of arrival the four vailxi fighters were released to escort the transports.

******

They arrived on schedule; before first light. Hovering over the city of Mohenjo-Daro the ships waited for daylight so that they could see where they would be landing.

******

At dawn the order to land was given and the six ships headed for a field on the south side of the Citadel. The transports landed first and the fighters came to rest by their sides.

The citizens of Mohenjo-Daro had been observing the ships while they hovered over the city, and as soon as the ships landed everybody ran toward where they landed.

An awesome display of technical superiority, nothing like this had ever been seen by these people.

General Khun and the ambassador waited by the transports. Eventually, a court official showed up and the ambassador requested an audience with the Rishi-King.

Khun and the ambassador were escorted to the Citadel while the rest of the soldiers and the officers remained by the ships.

The Citadel was a fortress built over a mound forty feet higher than the surrounding land. The steep ground disruption served as vertical walls.

Once on the other side of the Citadel South Gate they went up a long flight of stairs that led to the Assembly Hall. While they went up the stairs General Khun noticed a fortified building to his right; it was the army garrison that protected the Citadel; from its watchtower – taller than the fortress walls – some soldiers were observing what was happening at the landing site.

The Rishi-King living quarters were by the Assembly Hall. Their escort took them to the Assembly Hall and then went over to report to the king that he had visitors.

When informed about the visitors the king ordered that they be invited to share his breakfast table, and for them to wait in the Banquet Room.

While waiting, the general and the ambassador had been trying to memorize the layout of the Citadel. The Assembly Hall was about a hundred feet long; had thirty columns; five rows of six; spaced about sixteen feet apart.

To the northeast, the city and the river were seen from their vantage point. To the south, the field where the ships rested was also visible.

Their escort came back; he conveyed the king's message, "The king will see you. You are invited to share his breakfast table. Please follow me; I'll take you to the Banquet Room where he will soon join you."

The man escorted the visitors and left them at the Banquet Room; the room was almost as large as the Assembly Hall; but it had no pillars. On the east side of the room there was a very large semi-circular table almost as wide as the room.

The general and the ambassador waited; and while doing so studied the symbols on the walls and wondered about their meanings; for sure religious symbols, they thought.

A short time later the Rishi-King made his entrance with two of his assistant priests.

After the usual introductions they sat at the table; the king at the head of the table, and following the established protocol; the ambassador on his right side, the general on his left side, and the king assistants by the sides of the visitors.

One of the assistants rang a bell and three servants entered the room bearing trays of fruits and what looked like some kind of cereal.

While they ate their breakfast the king asked the visitors, "How was your trip?"

The general saw an opening, a chance to assess the king reactions; so he answered, "It was an uneventful trip, our ships didn't run into any problems; but, we can't say the same for a village that we saw on the other side of your Western frontier. Fires were seen on the ground, houses were burning. The illumination from the fires gave us a clue of what was happening; the streets were littered with debris. It was evident that the village had been looted; most likely by one of the nomad tribes that roam your Western frontier. Are you not afraid that someday they may attack one of your villages?"

"It will never happen," the king answered. "They know that we are a peaceful kingdom, and that if we ever have to defend our territory, because of our large army; they would be destroyed. They have never bothered us."

The general concluded that they better start looking for the king replacement.

They finished eating. The servants cleared the table, and then the king asked, "Well...how can we be of service?"

The ambassador answered, "Our Air Assault Forces are on a training mission. Because they will be visiting many countries it was decided that I should accompany them; that will give me an opportunity to offer and negotiate new trade or protection treaties.

"We need to purchase fresh fruits and other perishables and would appreciate if we could do so during the day and depart tomorrow at first light."

The king answered, "Of course, you are more than welcome to stay. You can send your men to the public market to purchase whatever you need. And tonight, you and your officers are invited to dinner here at the Citadel. You will have an opportunity to talk to the prominent merchants and to see if they have a product that may interest you or if you have something that may interest them."

"Yes we can do that," the ambassador said.

The king added, "All of your men are also invited to visit our city, they may want to purchase some souvenirs at the bazaars. By the way, how many of you will there be for dinner tonight?"

"There will be five of us," the ambassador answered.

The king then said, "Well, I imagine that there is a lot that you have to take care of; among other things, to resupply your ships. So, we'll expect you and your officers here at sundown."

General Khun and the ambassador returned to the landing site where the rest of the men waited.

The three officers at the landing site approached the general and the ambassador and one of them asked, "Well, how did it go?"

The general answered, "So far so good, except that we may be in the market for a new Rishi-King."

"Why is that?" another of the officers asked.

The general answered, "The king is under the impression that the nomad tribes would not dare to attack his kingdom.

"Tonight, we are invited to dinner; that's when we'll propose our Military Protection Treaty to the king; and then we'll know if a change of leadership is needed."

The general and the officers then accompanied a group of soldiers to the city, and while the soldiers went to the market square to purchase the necessary supplies, the general and the officers reconnoitered the city; they were looking for the army garrison but none of the buildings within the city walls looked like what a military garrison should look like, and no soldiers were to be seen.

Just before the transports landed the general had noticed some large buildings by the riverside so he asked one of the residents about the buildings; the man told him one of the buildings was the army garrison and that the other buildings were used to store their weapons and other military supplies.

It makes sense, the general thought. The river splits the kingdom all the way to the ocean. The garrison being by the riverside would speed up the loading of the soldiers and their weapons if they have to be deployed to other regions.

Before landing he had noticed that there was a short waterway that ended up at the longest one of the buildings; that's where they must have the barges needed to transport the soldiers and their weapons; and it is a safe bet to assume that the heavy weapons and supplies are already loaded.

Having seen all they needed to see the general and the officers returned to the landing site.

Upon their return the officers allowed groups of soldiers to visit the city so that they would be familiar with the city layout; in case they have to go in to neutralize any military opposition.

There was nothing else to do but wait for the sun to disappear over the Western horizon.

CHAPTER 17

Kalac arrived at the base in the afternoon and gave   Torr some final instructions.

Torr waited; his departure must be timed so as to reach the approach position just before first light, he can't take a chance of being detected if he has to hover in place for a long time.

"At last," Torr said when a light started to blink on the control panel; the navigational system was telling him that it was time to leave.

Torr took to the air and headed east, gradually gaining altitude, reaching out for the programmed altitude; once there; twelve miles high, a canopy of twinkling stars overwhelmed his senses, and he imagined himself as one among the stars.

Due to his relative low altitude and high speed the ship was leaving a visible streak of light behind due to the friction generated by its force field as it deflected the atmosphere.

A sailor on a ship below his flight path happened to be observing the night sky and saw a shooting star; it traced an arc across the starred sky disappearing over the Eastern horizon.

******

An hour after departure he found himself a hundred miles of the coast of Poseidia and according to the navigational system aligned with the outpost. Torr proceeded to take the ship down to sea level and almost skimming the ocean waves headed for the two mountains and the large brook that would guide him to the outpost. He entered the gorge formed by the two mountains, found the brook, and followed it all the way to its origin.

The granite mountain with the sheer vertical cliff was now in front of him; then, he ascended looking for the shelf where the entrance to the cave was located; found it, stopped, checked the skies for any ships flying overhead, and then activated the signal that would open the door. A short time after, the wall in front of him yielded its secret; a cave materialized; it emerged from the bowels of the granite mountain. He entered the cave and as soon as the ship came to rest on the ground the door closed.

Daylight turned into darkness, so Torr turned the ship lights on, and then waited.

Eventually, the cave lights were turned on and a man dressed as an Atlantean farmer entered the cave; it was the priest. Torr secured the ship, picked up his bag, and came out of the ship. The man waited by the door; Torr went over to where he was and said, "My name is Torr."

"I am Ralh," the priest said. "We received a coded signal advising us about your arrival today. Did you bring what I ordered?"

"Yes I did, let me get it."

Torr returned to the ship and came back with a package.

Ralh examined the contents, and then said, "Spare parts for my crystal generators. Please follow me."

They left the cave. Ralh locked the door and turned the lights off from the tunnel side.

During the time that it took to ride the electric pod to the house Torr briefed Ralh on what was expected of him.

The tunnel was about three miles long; and at the end, another security door identical to the one at the secret base; on the other side, the house cellar.

When they entered the house the first thing that Ralh did was to tell his wife that he must accompany Torr to Semira and that they would be leaving right after breakfast.

At breakfast they talked about Muror and about what was happening in the rest of the world; after exhausting the topic Torr asked, "How does your lives differ from ours in the Motherland?"

"The hardest thing," Ralh answered, "is that we can't have any descendants; but, that is how it has to be, we volunteered for the job and knew what to expect."

"Do you ever get to see your parents?" Torr asked.

"We keep in touch," Ralh said. "Written notes are exchanged when the Archpriest pilots resupply the outpost. Once a year we are taken to the Great Temple where we spend a whole day with our parents. While at the temple we can't leave its premises. Since we can't stay away from the farm for more than two consecutive days we fly back the next day.

"Our families are told that we are assigned as observers on a foreign land and that for our safety the location can't be revealed."

"What...if one of you die?" Torr asked.

"In that case," Ralh answered, "the surviving one goes back to Muror and will serve as an assistant to the Great Temple Personnel Overseer. The neighbors are told that the farm was sold and a new young couple will take over; that will also be the case if we become too old to take care of the farm or for me to visit the Semira market place."

"How do you keep up with what is happening in the Atlantean Empire?" Torr asked.

Ralh answered, "A few times a month I go to Semira to sell my farm produce and you will be surprised as to how much you can learn from the merchants of the other kingdoms. I also intercept and decode the military radiated signals."

After finishing their breakfast Torr said, "I have to be in Semira by tonight; is that possible? Can it be done?"

Ralh answered, "Not on my cart, it would take two days; but, we can do it if we use the waterway boat; that by the way will go by our waterway dock in about an hour. It takes about half-an-hour to walk to the dock, so let's get ready. You better change into whatever disguise you are planning on using. What would it be?"

Torr answered, "I was planning on dressing as a sailor during my stay in Semira. What do you suggest?"

Ralh answered, "If we are using the boat there is no way that you can dress as a sailor. The boat captain will start questioning you about what is the name of the ship that you sail on, and about the ports that you have visited. It would be too risky. You better dress as a merchant during the trip to Semira. Did you bring a merchant costume with you?"

"Yes I did. Kalac insisted that I bring along a Murovian merchant tunic in case I needed to visit specific areas where a sailor would be seen as out of place. I have the two outfits here in my bag; the merchant and the sailor outfits."

"Well...it looks as if you will be able to make it to Semira by tonight, so hurry up and change into your merchant costume, and leave here what you are wearing now."

Ralh went to pack a bag for the two days he will stay in Semira, and Torr went to another room to change into his new disguise.

When Torr emerged from the room Ralh handed Torr a small glass jar in a pouch and said, "Here's this, take it with you; you'll need it."

Torr looked at the jar then asked, "What is this...and what is it for?"

"It is a temporary blondish dye for your hair; you need it, that is, if you want to pass for an Atlantean sailor. You will never convince anybody with your dark hair."

"How do I apply it?" Torr asked.

Ralh explained, "Smear a small amount on your hair and then with wet fingers disperse the dye to color all your hair."

Torr then asked, "How can I remove it?"

"It's easy," Ralh answered. "It will come off by rubbing your hair under a stream of water, so stay away from the rain, and make sure you don't fall into the waterways."

Torr asked, "I see that the two of you have blond hair. Do you dye your hair?"

The wife answered, "Yes we do, but we use a permanent dye and it is waterproof...it lasts about a month."

Torr put the jar away in his bag and said, "I have used a disguise before but not in Semira, I guess that makes a difference."

"Yes it does, now...let's go," Ralh said.

On their way to the waterway Ralh briefed Torr on what was happening in Semira; he told him, "As far as I know, two days ago two transports left Semira – fully loaded including four vailxi – with half of their Air Assault Forces on board; destination unknown. I doubt it is a training mission, an ambassador is accompanying them.

"Last night I intercepted and decoded a message from their fleet. At the end of the transmission somebody in Semira asked the ambassador if he made contact; the answer was yes. No further dialogue as to what 'contact' refers to. Do you have any idea about what is going on?"

Torr thought about it for a moment, and then said, "There is a possible connection with what I'm investigating. They may be trying to intimidate some other kingdoms.

"Do you know in which direction they headed for after their take-off; east or west?"

"No way to know unless you witnessed the take-off," Ralh said, "but I'm sure that you can find out at the air base."

Torr then said, "We'll do that as soon as we get to Semira. If I'm not mistaken there are civilian flights operating on the western side of the air base. Is that so?"

"Yes, that is correct," Ralh said. "There are daily flights to the other capital cities of Atlantis.

"The ships look like the military transports except that they are much smaller versions and designed for carrying cargo and civilian passengers."

While they walked they talked some more about what to expect and what to do upon reaching Semira.

They reached the waterway. A short time later a boat appeared on the western horizon. It was odd, Torr thought, no sails or oars were visible; yet the boat was moving at a relatively fast rate of speed; for a moment it baffled him; but, after thinking it over he concluded that most likely a mercury power plant was being used, so he exclaimed, "Amazing! They are using mercury power plants to power their boats; the same type used in the airships."

"That is partially true," Ralh said.

"What do you mean?" Torr asked.

Ralh answered, "Well...it is true that they use a mercury power plant but on this application the mercury vapors are not fed to a vortex coil."

"Then, how does it work?" Torr asked.

Ralh explained, "The mercury vapors are fed to a sealed chamber; inside, there is a wheel with deflecting cavities on its periphery. The wheel will rotate when the mercury vapors impact the deflectors. There is a special coupling system to insure that there are no mercury vapor losses for there is a long shaft sticking out of the sealed chamber; one side is joined to the wheel and the other end to a screw-shaped disk. When the screw is rotating it displaces the water to the rear and the boat will move forward."

"I see," Torr said; then questioned, "How come they use a power plant like that in the waterway boats and not in their ocean-going ships?"

Ralh explained, "To be able to deliver the goods and the passengers, on a timely fashion, to the different cities and villages you must have a reliable on-time transport system; that can't be done if you were to depend on the wind. As to why the mercury power plants are not used to power the ocean-going ships that ply the world oceans; they don't want the technology to fall in the wrong hands. All the components of the power plant are sealed in a box; the only thing sticking out is a shaft. The mechanics at the air base; the ones that build and service the mercury power plants are the only ones authorized to open the box if repairs are needed."

The boat came to a stop alongside the dock and the two of them climbed aboard.

There were three passengers aboard; farmers; and like the boat captain they knew Ralh. After the usual greetings the captain remarked, "I see that you are not going to the market place today."

"No, this time I'm visiting Semira with my friend," and as he said that he gave Torr a slap on his back; then told him, "Follow me."

Torr followed Ralh all the way to the front benches, away from the other three passengers and the captain that were at the rear of the boat.

Once they were seated Ralh explained his seat selection, "The main reason; I don't want them to hear our conversation, also you are dressed as a Murovian merchant and they would start asking questions that only a real merchant would know.

"Their crops are citrus fruits. They export dry fruits to the other Atlantean kingdoms. I'm sure that before our trip is over they will come over and start asking if you are interested in the products that they export; if that happen tell them that you are not familiar with the import-export trade, that you are a shopkeeper back home, and that you are visiting friends.

"Like them, I grow citrus fruits but because I need an excuse to visit Semira about twice a month I also plant short term crops; like vegetables. When I take the citrus fruits to the market place I use my cart, and for my vegetables; I use the waterway boat."

"After what I have seen so far," Torr said, "I believe that returning by boat is not an option for I will return dressed as a sailor."

"Why is that so?" Ralh asked.

"To do what I have in mind I must dress as an Atlantean sailor, so, when we get to Semira we have to find a safe place where I can dye my hair, change into the sailor's outfit, and get rid of what I'm wearing. Do you know of a place where I can do that?"

"Yes, I think I do." Ralh answered; then asked, "Why are you getting rid of what you are wearing now?"

Torr answered, "A Sailors' Inn is not a safe place to leave a bag with your belongings while you are out all day. Somebody could open it to see if there is anything worth stealing; if that was to happen and he discovers what I'm wearing now in the bag he may suspect that the owner is a spy and report it to the authorities; anonymously of course. In Semira you will stay overnight in the inn where the farmers usually stay, as for myself, I will stay at a Sailors' Inn."

"I see that you are planning on visiting some specific places in Semira," Ralh said.

"You are quite right," Torr said, "To carry out my plan I have to be able to access some areas where I must blend with the sailors.

"As I told you, on my return trip I will be dressed as a sailor; an Atlantean one. Returning by boat is out. If any of the passengers on this trip or the captain happen to be on-board the day I return they will recognize me."

"Yes," Ralh said. "I can imagine what could happen."

"I'm sure," Torr said, "that they would report the anomaly to the authorities; they saw us together and you told them that I was your friend, you would be interrogated and submitted to a brain scan."

"I was trained to resist a brain scan," Ralh said, "but even if they can't find me guilty of any wrongdoing it could endanger our outpost. I would probably end up being a marked man; their police force would keep an eye on me and my farm from then on."

"We agree," Torr said. "So, I'm afraid that to be on the safe side the only other choice is to use the road when I return. As far as I know the road that we happen to be looking at goes all the way to Semira. Is that so?"

"Yes it does," Ralh answered.

While they talked Torr had been observing the road. On a forested land next to Ralh's farm a logging operation was in progress. Elephants were carrying logs and depositing them by the waterway lay-by where a barge was being loaded.

Torr noticed some buildings near the waterway; for sure the business office and the workers' living quarters; that gave him an idea, so he asked, "Can a chariot be hired to bring me to the logging camp?"

"Yes, of course," Ralh said. "That is, if you don't mind enduring the rattling noise and jolts as the chariot bounces over the stone blocks."

"To return I will have to hire a chariot," Torr said, "but instead of going all the way to your farm I will have the driver drop me off at the logging camp; that way the driver or the agent at the rental office would never know my true final destination. I estimate that I would have to walk for about three hours to reach your farm."

"That is about right – three hours, I think," Ralh said; then added, "There is only one boat a day scheduled from and to Semira on this route; the one coming from Semira departed just before first light; in about three hours you will hear its howling horn.

"I suggest that you wait about an hour after the boat departure before you show up at the chariot rental agency."

"Why is that?" Torr asked.

Ralh answered, "So that it would be impossible to catch up with the boat at the first canal junction; the boat stops there for about half an hour to load the supplies ordered by the shopkeepers on this route.

"If you show up at the chariot rental agency before the boat stops at the first canal junction the agent will inform you that it is possible, using a chariot, to catch up with the boat at the first junction.

"After the first stop it would be impossible to catch up with the boat and that would leave only one option if for some reason you can't wait till next day; rent a chariot; but if you try to do so you better have a credible need or the agent may start questioning your motives for people very seldom rent a chariot to travel that far. Not only would it take much longer than the boat but it is an exhausting proposition. Also, the main reason; it will cost a lot more; in your case, probably over fifty times the boat fare.

"If you don't justify your request he may suspect that you are running away from something – maybe the authorities? And who knows, because you are a stranger he may decide to report you to the nearest army guard station; that by the way is not that far from the rental agency."

"Yes...I see what the probabilities of being discovered are; to prevent that I have to be one step ahead," Torr said; then asked, "So, any ideas?"

Ralh was silent for some time, thought about it, then smiled and broke the silence, "I think that I have a good one. Tell the agent that you missed the boat departure that morning and that it is imperative that you deliver a scroll and talk to a relative that works at the logging camp before you ship out next day in the late afternoon. That the scroll has to do with an inheritance."

"Yes, that should do it," Torr said. "The reason for renting the chariot is credible and what I would be wearing will validate the impersonation; an Atlantean sailor."

Ralh added, "Tell the agent that it is a one way trip. That you will stay overnight and return in the morning boat so that you can be back on time to ship out. And something else; do you have enough coins to pay for all that you may need?"

"Yes I do," Torr answered.

"Because of the distance," Ralh said, "I estimate that you will arrive at the logging camp about an hour before sundown. Unlike the winding waterways of Muror the Poseidia ones and their parallel roads run in straight lines, hence the light torches are further apart. So, you will have to walk for some time in partial darkness, and then there are no lights once you leave the main road and enter the road that leads to my farm."

"That would not be a problem," Torr said. "The moon will light the way."

"You hope; what if clouds cover the moon?" Ralh asked.

"If that was the case I can manage," Torr said. "Before I left Muror I memorized the maps of this region."

They left the forested area behind; vast cultivated plains were visible on both sides of the waterway.

Torr noticed some workers planting a new crop in one of the fields; there was something odd about their behavior; they seemed to move and interact in a sluggish way, so he asked, "Are they the 'things'?"

"Yes they are," Ralh said; then asked, "Have you ever seen one of them before?"

"No, this is my first time," Torr said.

******

What they were seeing were not pre-paid workers called slaves in Muror, these were truly slaves; genetic humanoids created to satisfy the Atlanteans worldly desires. Most of the people of Atlantis intended to live an effortless life, a life of easy and pleasure.

A long time ago, by using genetic manipulation they created a race of humanoids devoid of spiritual awareness or rationality; beings that depended on their masters for all their needs.

They were used mostly in farms and as house servants.

******

Torr felt pity for the 'things' and imagined life as perceived by their minds; a meaningless existence, like the sense of awareness of inanimate matter and all low level life that comprises the universe; only an awareness of being so that they can exist to serve and act as a backdrop in God's electrical picture-play.

Selfishness ruled the land of Atlantis.

Right after going by the field where the 'things' were working they came across an irrigation canal junction.

Ralh asked, "Do you see the large building by the canal sluice?"

"Yes...I see it," Torr answered.

"Well," Ralh said, "that's where the sluice operator lives. The building also serves as an inn; two rooms are available. A likely place for the chariot driver to spend the night on his way back to Semira."

The boat slowed down; once secured to the dock two farmers came aboard; each one dragging a two-wheeled small cart full of fruits and vegetables, on their way to the Semira market place.

The farmers went to the rear of the boat and secured the carts, then, they sat by the other three farmers. It didn't take long, the five of them decided to go over to talk with the foreign merchant that was traveling with Ralh.

When Ralh saw that the farmers were heading their way he said, "Oh that does it, from now on we won't be able to talk about your mission."

"That's for sure," Torr said with a smile on his face.

Torr, of course; told them that he was a shopkeeper and was not familiar with the import-export business; hearing that, you could see the farmers disappointment expressed in their faces; but, they didn't go back to their original seats at the back of the boat, and from then on engaged in the usual trivial conversation generated by the visible environment.

From then on Torr kept an eye on the road landmarks.

It was a clear morning, clouds were beginning to form. From their actual position they could see over the horizon the peaks of the Granite Mountains that encircled Semira.

******

Poseidia, like the other four islands of Atlantis enjoyed a subtropical climate. About half of Poseidia was covered by densely forested plains where wild animals were hunted.

The cultivated plains were dotted with wooded knolls that rose above ground level; they provided the farmers with the habitat needed for their domesticated animals.

The flat lands of Poseidia were strewn with small lakes and swampy regions.

The rivers flowing down from the mountains emptied into the main waterways and by means of sluices the water was fed and retained in the smaller secondary canals called irrigation canals that crisscross the plains; the water on these canals used to irrigate the crops in the summer; the dry season. In the winter they relied mostly on rainfall. The irrigation canals also served as a link to the faster and larger main waterway boats.

The flat lands of Poseidia were no more than twenty feet above sea level; the Acropolis was about 200 feet above sea level and the rest of the city of Semira about thirty feet above the sea.

******

Three hours after their first stop an intermittent howling horn was heard, it was the other boat. The captain of their boat replied with the same. Both boats slowed down as they passed by, then they accelerated again and retook their pace.

They already went by eight docks; eight more to go before they reach Semira. If there are no passengers at a stop and they don't have any deliveries to make they don't   stop; like when they went by the logging camp dock, there was nothing to pick up or to deliver.

Semira was only four hours away; they will arrive by midafternoon.

CHAPTER 18

At Mohenjo-Daro the sun was about to relinquish its throne to the shadows of darkness.

The soldiers that went to the city were back and Khun and the three officers were about to leave for the Citadel. The ambassador, as planned, had gone ahead; his intention; to befriend the priests and to assess which one was the ideal candidate to replace the Rishi-King if he didn't agree with what they were going to propose.

General Khun and the three officers left the landing site and headed for the Citadel; once there they went up a long flight of stairs; at the end they turned left and went straight to the Banquet Room. They went in, there were about fifty guests in the room; most of them gathered in small groups.

The general saw the ambassador; he was amid a larger group that if what they were wearing was an indication of their status in life they must be the rich merchants; probably inquiring about new trade possibilities.

Khun and the officers joined the ambassador group.

Yes, they were the rich merchants.

The officers then became the center of interest to the group. That gave Khun and the ambassador an opportunity to break away from the group; they needed to talk in private.

When alone with the ambassador the general asked, "Have you found the candidate to replace the king if needed be?"

"Yes, I think we have our man; he is one of the priests invited to the banquet," the ambassador said as he glanced in the priest direction.

The general looked at the priest, then asked, "Are you sure that he agrees with what we propose?"

"Oh yes," the ambassador said. "He is an ambitious priest and is of the opinion that it would be a good idea to have a protection treaty considering their primitive army. He said that if it was up to him he would sign a treaty; reading between the lines he meant...if I was the king!"

"Well...that was easy," the general said. "Now we must convince the Rishi-King; and I suspect that this is not going to be an easy task if what we heard this morning is still his point of view. Something tells me that he wouldn't change his mind.

"Whoever is the king will be told about the 'extra' payments once the proposal is accepted."

On their way to join the officers Khun noticed a man in uniform so he asked the ambassador, "Is that a general?"

"Yes, and he is the one in charge of the army garrison and the military forces in the region," the ambassador said.

"The Gods are on our side," Khun said. "Go back and join the officers. I have to talk to the general and convince him that it is for the good of their country to be protected by a military treaty. I want him on our side."

Khun than went over to where the general was and told him, "We need to talk in private."

They left the room, and then Khun asked, "Have you had any of your villages raided by the nomad tribes that roam your Western frontier?"

"No...So far," the general answered.

"The reason I ask," Khun said, "is because on our way here we saw a village being plundered on the other side of your Western frontier."

"They have never bothered us," the general said. "I guess because we have an army and outnumber them."

"I imagine that you have a small number of soldiers patrolling your borders," Khun said, "but your main forces are stationed here; it will take a long time for them to be deployed and by the time you do so it will be too late.

"Due to the land topographical features it is easier for the nomad tribes to attack the villages on the other side. But, what do you think will happen if they run out of villages to plunder on their side; would they attack yours?"

"Yes...I imagine it could happen," the general said.

"It is not a case of it could happen," Kun said, "but when will it happen. They know that they can get away with it, that by the time your army arrives they will be gone; out of reach on the other side of the frontier.

"There is one thing that you have to consider; you are in charge of the army and will be held responsible for whatever happen. Your job will be in jeopardy.

"On the other hand, if the king were to sign a treaty we can wipe out the invaders before they can do any damage to the villages or the farms."

"But, how can that be possible, you being so far away?" the general asked.

"If the king signs the treaty," Khun said, "we will install code transmitters on your frontier outposts; they will have to be located in key spots; like mountain trails and roads that lead to the villages and farms. I have seen in the maps that your villages and farmlands, because of the terrain features, are not that close to the frontier; they are over an hour away by horseback; the raiders mode of transport. Our vailxi fighters will intercept the raiders just before they reach the villages or your farms."

"Are they that fast?" the general questioned.

"Yes they are," Khun answered.

"If that is true," the general said, "it is a brilliant defensive scheme – I like it."

"Yes, it is true and feasible," Khun said, "but your king is convinced that your kingdom is safe, that the vandals will never attack your villages because you are a peaceful people; that's what he told us this morning.

"What he is not aware is that the nomad tribes are running out of villages to plunder on the other side and to subsist they will have to cross your frontier and attack your villages and farms."

"The truth is that I never thought that it could happen," the general said.

"Well, it will eventually happen," Khun said, "and you will be blamed for not being prepared."

"What can I do to help?" the general asked.

"Tonight, we need you to help us convince the king that he should sign a Military Protection Treaty so that the ones that live close to the Western frontier will be protected from the vandals." Khun said.

"But...what if he doesn't sign?" the general asked.

"In that case," Khun said, "it is obvious that you need a new king; one that cares about what could happen to his subjects and his kingdom."

The general couldn't believe what he just heard, so he asked, "What are you suggesting? You are not thinking...?"

Khun interrupted the general and said, "No, No, it's not what you think, you can exile him if he refuses to protect the kingdom. I'm sure that we can find a priest that does care about the inhabitants of the Western frontier.

"Believe me; we have seen what is happening on the other side of the border. One day they will do the same on your side.

"Tonight, we'll see if our proposal is accepted."

The general realized that he found himself at the crossroads of an important decision that could impact the kingdom submissive psyche, so he said, "I find myself in a difficult position. On one hand I must be loyal to my king, but on the other hand I am responsible for the safety of the kingdom.

"As I see it, we have two options. One is to accept your proposal; it would be cheaper and our soldiers would not have to risk their lives. The other option is quite expensive; I would have to relocate half my troops to patrol the Western frontier; that also entails the relocation of their families and the construction of fort-outposts."

"There is one thing I want to know," Khun said; then asked, "Will you order your men to stand down if we deem necessary to replace the Rishi-King?"

The general didn't answer right away; he seemed to be evaluating his options. After thinking it over, he answered, "Well...I agree with you that it would be the thing to do if we want to protect our kingdom, so, I have decided to hold back my troops. Anyway, it would be stupid of me to oppose your forces. I'm aware of what your weapons can do."

"A wise decision," Khun said. "Not only would we be protecting your people but also your crops in that region. Most of the spices you use and the ones that you export, because of the soil and climatic requirements, are grown and harvested close to the Western frontier."

It was getting to be about time for the king to make his appearance, so, the generals decided to go back to the Banquet Room.

When General Khun entered the room he saw the officers and the ambassador huddled together at the back of the room, they had been exchanging information about what was learned while interacting with the other guests; so he headed their way. When Khun joined the group the ambassador asked, "Well, how did it go?"

Khun answered, "We have him on our side. Their army will stand down if we have to replace their king; that means no ground operations losses; this was not envisioned in our operational plan."

"That's good news," the ambassador said. "No losses to report when we get back."

Right after the ambassador remarks the king and three other priests entered the room, and one of the priests said, "Please take your places."

The king sat at the head of the table; his entourage and his general to his left, the visitors to his right.

The rest of the guests approached the table; once they were seated one of the priests rang a bell and the servants made their entrance carrying large trays. Drinks and exotic foods were placed on the table, by the looks of it; a banquet it was.

For the first course the visitors were served a soup with a floating object on it. One of the officers scooped the round object and was about to put it in his mouth when he noticed that it looked like an eye, an eye!!! Startled by the find he started to ask, ""What...?"

General Khun didn't let him finish and told him, "Don't say anything, just leave it alone, put it back and eat the rest of the soup."

The officer looked at the general with not so friendly eyes and gritting his teeth did as ordered; the other two officers and the ambassador did as suggested. Offending their host was not an option.

During the meal the guests engaged in the usual trivial conversation heard in such gatherings.

Once they finished eating and drinking the table was cleared.

Then, the Atlantean ambassador introduced the subject matter of the nomad tribes; he presented the story they had told the king that morning, and then explained to the guests what they were proposing; a Military Protection Treaty.

When the ambassador finished explaining what the treaty was all about a pro and con discussion ensued among the guests present; most of them were merchants, so, of course, they were for the treaty, for most of the herbs and spices they export and sell in their country are grown close to the Western frontier.

A spokesman representing the merchants asked the king, "Would you sign such a treaty?"

The king answered, "No, I wouldn't sign such a treaty, we don't need a protection treaty, we have an army," then looking at his general asked him, "What do you think?"

The general answered, "We have an army, but, a one hour response time would be impossible to achieve under the present conditions; the cost would be prohibitive. Half our army would have to be transferred to the Western frontier and a large number of forts would have to be built, also we would have to provide housing for the soldiers' families.

"Their protection treaty sounds reasonable to me. A plus factor would be that our present army could still be used as we use it today; to provide the security in the central regions of the kingdom. To patrol the frontier would be too costly and inefficient due to the fact that the nomad tribes are constantly on the move and we can't predict where they would strike next. We don't have airships, it would be impossible to transport the soldiers in one hour from the garrisons to where the crossing is taking place. That is my opinion," the general said.

The Rishi-King thought about it for a short time and then said, "I think that all of you are mistaken, they have never attacked us and I think that they never will." having said that and facing the guests added, "I thank you for coming and bid you good night." then he stood up and with his escorts left the room.

The guests left the room shaking their heads.

General Khun, his officers and the ambassador left the Citadel and headed for the landing field where the ships rested; once there Khun ordered the officers to double the guard and to have the soldiers ready for action before first light. They will attack the Citadel right after sunrise.

CHAPTER 19

Three hours had gone by - the next stop; the cargo stop where Ralh was planning on getting off the boat. They can't go all the way to the end of the waterway; that's where the chariot rental agency and the boat agency are located.

Being so close to Semira was a spectacle by itself. The mountains that surrounded the city on three sides – because of a lack of a gradual transition between the flat land and their tops – made you feel like if you were looking up at the sky from inside the bowels of the planet; it was a majestic sight, the sheer cliffs.

Ralh waited until they reached the cargo dock and as soon as they tie down the boat he told Torr, "Here is where we get off the boat, so let's go."

Torr followed Ralh who headed for a public bathhouse that was close by. A man was coming out when they entered the bathhouse. They were lucky, the place was empty. Ralh gave Torr a small leather pouch and told him, "Enter one of the stalls, change your outfit and use the blond dye, there is some water in the pouch I just gave you."

Not long after – an Atlantean sailor emerged.

Now they had to get rid of the tunic. Ralh found an isolated place on a park and with a knife shredded the tunic and dumped the pieces in a trash bin.

They were ready.

It was midafternoon – the first thing they had to do was to find a place to stay.

Ralh went first to the inn where he stays while in Semira when he uses the boat, rented a room and left his bag; once that was done they headed for the Large Port; that's where most of sailors' inns were located; there Torr rented a room and left his bag.

Now Ralh must teach Torr how to interact with the city. The first lesson - how to get to the air base. There was a monorail station near the Sailors' Inn and while they walked over to the station Ralh explained the essentials with regard to the use of the monorail transport system.

It didn't take long to board one of the electric pods that were heading for the air base; on their way Torr was able to see the peoples' materialistic psyche expressed.

The way people dressed diverged from what the rest of the people in the planet were accustomed to; the women wore gloves, blouses, short pants, and mid-calf leather boots.

As for the men; some of them wore tunics; like the priests, the rich and the government high officials. The rest of the men; like the common citizens, and the soldiers; wore short pants, shirts, jackets, and boots. All of the men that Torr had seen so far were wearing mid-calf black leather boots. The soldiers he had seen carried their short swords attached to a belt in the waist.

They were heading to the east, toward the granite mountain where the air base was located.

The monorail ran parallel to a road that also ended up at the base, so Torr focused his interest on the road; he was trying to familiarize himself with the location of the buildings or farms along the way; you never know, one day he may have to use that road.

Upon reaching the base they went directly to the ticket office of the civilian terminal where Ralh inquired about the flights to Gades; he was informed that the next flight would be departing next morning, at sunrise; he knew that, but by asking about it gave them a reason for being there.

When they left the ticket office Ralh noticed a man that was cleaning the building windows, he went over to where he was and asked him, "Do you know from what gate does the flight to Gades leaves in the morning?"

"Yes, the number four boarding gate." the man said.

Then Ralh mentioned, "I heard that military exercises are going on, that two of our transports full of soldiers left the field and headed south."

"Well, I don't know anything about military exercises, but they didn't go south; the two military ships headed in an eastern direction when they left the base; I saw them leaving as I arrived at the base in the morning."

That's what they needed to know.

As they walked away from the man Ralh told Torr, "It's not a military exercise; if it was, they would have gone south as they always do.

They went back to Semira – there was about half-an-hour of daylight left so Ralh took Torr on a tour of the city commercial area that existed in-between the Large Port and the Small Port; that's where many of the businesses and some of the government offices where located.

After having something to eat they agreed to meet in front of the Sailors' Inn where Torr was staying; right after sunrise.

CHAPTER 20

At Mohenjo-Daro the sun overtook darkness; it was time; time to do what they came to do.

The fighter pilots were standing by in their vailxi, ready to protect the transports and the soldiers. They will stay on the ground for if their general honors the agreement that his army will stand down they wouldn't be needed.

General Khun briefed the officers and the ambassador; to the ambassador he told, "We'll position our troops in front of the Citadel. You will enter the Citadel, request to talk to the Rishi-King; try to convince him of what could happen to his kingdom if he doesn't sign the treaty, and imply that the kingdom would be better off under a king that values the lives of his subjects.

"And of course, don't mention to the Rishi-King about our agreement with their general. If the king finds out that the general plans to hold back his troops he will have him arrested and appoint a replacement that will defend the Citadel; and that is not what we want.

"If everything works out according to our plan there shouldn't be any human losses; on neither side."

To the officers he told, "Position your troops facing the south gate; halfway from here to the Citadel, and then come back here."

The officers went over to comply with the order.

To the ambassador he told, "You can go now, request an audience with the king. We'll be here waiting for the king answer to our proposal."

The ambassador left for the Citadel; at the south gate he requested an audience with the king.

Not long after, a priest showed up and escorted the ambassador to the king's private office.

As soon as the ambassador entered the office the king said, "Please sit," and then asked. "What is happening? What can we do for you?"

The ambassador answered, "We'd like you to reconsider about the signing of the treaty."

"As I said before," the king said, "we don't need a treaty because the nomad tribes will never attack us."

"But, what if they do? Who will be to blame?" the ambassador asked; then added, "The merchants and the other guests that attended the banquet last night agreed that you should sign the treaty; why? Because not only would we be protecting the people but also the spices that you export; the ones that we buy from your merchants. We are sure that they would prefer to have a king that is willing to protect their interests and the lives of the people."

The king then said, "My advice to you; leave us alone and go back to Atlantis; or face the consequences. If you insist, we have no other choice but to destroy your leaders; and that means you and your officers. Your soldiers wouldn't be harmed, it's not their fault; they only obey orders."

"I will inform the general of your decision," the ambassador said; then left the Citadel.

The ambassador approached the general; and before he could say anything the general asked, "Well, how did it go?"

"Not so good," the ambassador said. "Not only does he refuses to sign a treaty but also threatened to destroy our leaders; he meant the five of us if we don't leave."

The five of them laughed at the suggestion.

General Khun was confident that they couldn't carry out the threat. It was evident that the king was not aware that the general would hold back the troops.

So, the order was given.

The three squadrons were deployed; their objective; the south gate of the Citadel.

In front of the troops; the three officers, while the general and the ambassador stayed behind.

The Rishi-King was informed by one of his assistants that the troops were moving, and in a collision course with the Citadel; to the king that meant that they were going to attack the Citadel.

The Rishi-King didn't want to do it, but there was no other solution.

What the Atlanteans didn't know and were about to find out was that the king was a Grand Master – and one of the few that could control matter with his mind.

The king found a high point from where he could see the advancing troops, then, he raised his hands to heaven and using his mental powers caused the ones that he had been in contact with – the ambassador, the general, and the tree officers – to drop dead.

The officers collapsed in front of the troops. When the soldiers saw the officers on the ground they looked to the rear and were surprised to see that the ambassador and the general were also laying on the ground.

Two healers – one from each ship – ran over to see what was wrong with the men – one went to the front, the other to the rear – they determined that the men were dead, dead!!! But how was that possible? No weapons were fired.

When the soldiers were told that the officers were dead they panicked and ran back to the transports.

The healers collected the bodies; took them to one of the transports and prepared them for the trip back to Semira – to their final resting place.

A discussion ensued as to what to do next, there were no officers to tell them what to do; they didn't know what they were supposed to be doing there.

The consensus was that the thing to do was to retreat, to get back to Semira as soon as possible, before the same thing happen to them.

The transports were loaded; then they took-off, and the vailxi followed the transports. Once in flight the vailxi were retrieved by the transports.

Then, a message was transmitted to Semira informing General Darko that they were returning to Semira, that all the officers and the ambassador were dead, and that there were no other losses.

They will be back at the base in about eighteen hours.

CHAPTER 21

A new day came to be. Torr and Ralh met in front of the Sailors' Inn.

Today, Ralh will familiarize Torr with the city, and decided to start by taking Torr to the Temple of Poseidon Plaza; that's where the Royal Palace was located.

A chariot was needed.

There were three chariot rental agencies in Semira and one of them was close by at the Small Port.

They rented the chariot and headed for the Acropolis. Ralh wanted to approach the Central Island from the south, so, using the Outer Wall Ring Road he circled the Three Ring Island on its east side; once he reached the South Bridge entry gate they had to park the chariot outside, the rest of the way they must walk. The only chariots allowed to enter the Three Ring Island were the ones used by the Royal Palace and the military, and most of the time they used the North Bridge; it led directly to the stables in the palace.

Torr and Ralh entered the island complex and after leaving the Race Course Island behind were on the causeway leading to the Grove of Poseidon Island; statues of Gods and kings lined both sides of the causeway. Once on the other side of the gate, on the island, Torr was overcome by a feeling of peace and tranquility; the place was full of small temples, fountains, and magnificent gardens that exuded a plethora of fragrances; undistinguished one from the other.

Leaving the Grove of Poseidon behind they entered the last causeway; the one that led to the Acropolis. When they entered the Acropolis Torr was awed by what he saw – the Temple of Poseidon; it was a colossal structure. The statue of Poseidon riding his chariot was almost as tall as a ten story building, and the cupola an extra 100 feet. The shiny yellow metal that covered the dome reflected the sun's rays from its surface – it was like a giant torch.

The plaza was surrounded by statues; but these ones unlike the ones in the causeway were colossal in size; perhaps to reflect the same symmetry of scale. There were two small temples in the plaza; on the east and the west side of the plaza – facing the front and the rear of the Temple of Poseidon. Visitors were seen going in and coming out of these two small temples. The Temple of Poseidon was off-limits to the general public.

The Royal Palace was on the north side of the temple and as they headed for the palace Ralh said, "The reason that we are here is so that you can see where the palace accesses are."

As they approached the palace Torr asked, "Are those stairs, one on each side, the main entrances?"

"Yes they are," Ralh answered; then added, "To your left, on the side of the building; that stair leads down to the stables and where they park the chariots. You have seen what the front of the palace looks like, so let's go to the Underground Docks; there are some stairs that go up to the palace; one of the them ends up in the kitchen that feeds the Royal Family; that's how the kitchen workers enter the palace; direct from the Underground Docks."

As they were leaving the Acropolis Torr asked, "What's inside the small temples?"

"The cold and warm water springs are housed in the temples," Ralh answered; then added, "The temple on your left houses the cold water spring, and the temple on your right the warm water spring. They supply all the water fit for drinking needed by the city of Semira. The warm water is also used in the Public Thermal Baths.

"An aqueduct – a tunnel – under the bridges roadway delivers the water to the city distribution network. The water flows by gravity – the Central Island; where the springs are, is almost 200 feet higher than the city."

They left the Three Ring Island, retrieved their chariot and drove to the Large Port where they found a boat that was about to leave for the Underground Docks; they took it; it was the same type of boat used in the waterways but smaller; powered by the mercury engines. To get across the Ring Islands there was a Subterranean Channel; during that portion of the trip – if it was a sailboat – horses on both sides of the channel pulled the boats from one Water Belt to the next, it was faster than using their oars.

When they entered the Underground Docks Torr was amazed at the size of the cave; it was about 700 feet deep and 1000 feet wide. Huge columns of solid stone were left standing during the construction of the cave; they went all the way up to the roof, about 100 feet.

Well over a hundred ships of all types – from warships to commercial vessels were under repair, serviced or under construction at the six wharves.

Torr was dressed as a sailor and Ralh as a farmer so they didn't look out of place among the rest of the people present; to others they were a farmer and a sailor probably looking for a commercial vessel.

There were some doors at the rear of the docks and as they went by them Ralh said, "Behind these doors are the stairs that go all the way to the palace, and the large one is where the steam powered elevator that the king uses is located."

"Yes, I've heard about his elevator and I can't blame him for using it. The Throne Room must be almost 300 feet above the docks." Torr said.

Ralh added, "There is a small steam powered elevator by the stairs that end up at the Royal Family kitchen; that's how they receive their food supplies."

Torr then noticed holes in the roof behind the solid stone columns at the rear of the cave so he asked, "What are those holes in the roof?"

"Oh...those are ventilation ducts that go all the way up to the palace."

"You don't say – interesting," Torr said.

Ralh then explained, "The sea breeze enters the huge cave and because of the air pressure differences the air flows to the top of the ducts and into the palace."

"Quite ingenious," Torr said; then thought that the ducts may come in handy; he could levitate and go up the ducts to listen to the conversations in the palace's offices; but he can't tell that to Ralh.

Ralh decided that Torr had seen all he needed to see so he said, "Let's go back, there must be a boat about ready to leave for the Large Port."

Back at the port, they retrieved the chariot and began their tour of the circular city.

Scores of soldiers were seen patrolling the city, specially the canal that led to the sea. At the end of the canal they stopped briefly at the first sluice gate to watch the parade of ships entering the canal from the ocean. Rippling waves lapped the canal stone walls as the ships went by. Some of them were using their sails; others were driven by their oarsmen.

A Trident – a symbol of the Royal House of Atlantis – adorned the face of the two gate-towers that controlled the sluice.

The rest of the morning they toured the city.

******

At noon they went back to the commercial section of the city – by the two ports – and returned the chariot to the rental agency.

******

After a lunch break Ralh said, "We'll stay in the area for the rest of the afternoon. If we don't learn anything new, then, your best bet would be the air base tomorrow. Also, you could try to befriend a palace worker; most of them live in the city and they commute every day, who knows what they may have heard."

The docks were full of vessels – they came from all over the world. The sounds of the different dialects and foreign languages created a cacophony of sounds unheard in any other place except at the docks.

They went over to the market square; during the time spent there they were unable to learn anything new, there was no clue as to the final destination of the military transports that left the air base.

As they went by a large building Ralh said, "That's the headquarters of the Poseidia Air Assault Forces."

Torr then said, "Somebody in there must be involved in the extortion plot that I'm investigating."

"That's for sure if they are using the military forces," Ralh said.

By the late afternoon Ralh had finished introducing Torr to the ways of the Atlanteans and how to interact with the city so he said, "Well...I think that you are ready to be by yourself, so I'll be leaving tomorrow morning, just before first light. I will meet you in front of the Sailors' Inn before I leave, in case you have to send any messages. Be outside waiting for me."

"I will be waiting," Torr said; then each one of them went back to the inn where they were staying.

CHAPTER 22

That same day – three hours after sundown; the two military transports with the Assault Forces on board landed at the base and the news of the death of the officers in charge spread like wildfire.

General Darko and the king had been informed when the transports left Mohenjo-Daro but it was kept a secret from the general public, but now, it was impossible to keep it a secret. The soldiers left the base and went home; and of course, told everybody they met about the way the officers died without a single shot being fired.

Just before midnight – the news reached the Sailors' Inn. The noisy disturbance created by intoxicated sailors returning to the inn woke up everybody; they were repeating aloud what they heard from the soldiers.

Torr went over to the front desk to find out what was happening and what he heard from the sailors was hard to believe. At Mohenjo-Daro; the Assault Forces were defeated, all the officers and the ambassador were killed, and the weird thing; the soldiers claimed that no weapons were used by the opposing army. The other thing that didn't make sense; the soldiers were not harmed. Why?

The puzzle was starting to unravel; Torr now knew where the Assault Forces had been; Mohenjo-Daro. Tomorrow will be a busy day. He will try to find out the names and positions of the dead officers, and if it was the same ambassador that went to Mayax. That will help him to identify the possible co-conspirators. But now he needed to sleep, he must get up before first light, he went back to his room.

******

In the morning; before first light, Torr as planned waited for Ralh in front of the Sailors' Inn.

When Ralh showed up Torr asked him, "Have you heard the news about their expeditionary force?"

"Yes, on my way here," Ralh said; then asked, "Is there a message that you want me to transmit to Muror when I get back home?

Torr replied, "Tell them about Mohenjo-Daro and what took place, and that I will try to link the dead officers and the ambassador to possible co-conspirators. That most likely I will return to Muror tomorrow."

Ralh then went over to the chariot rental agency and arranged to be driven to the western waterway boat dock.

Torr decided that his best option would be the palace ventilation ducts. Uranus; for sure, will interrogate the ones that had anything to do with the operation, and that would include the higher ranking soldiers that witnessed the death of their officers.

Torr headed straight for the Underground Docks; once there he went to the rear of the cave where the last row of columns and the ventilation ducts were located. Once he found what appeared to be the longest duct he stood against the back of the column and waited. The column was wide enough so that the people working on the ships couldn't see him. He looked left and right to make sure that he was the only one beyond the last line of columns; he was, so he initiated his ascent, went up the duct all the way to the opposite end. Iron bars covered the duct exit point, by what he could see he determined that the duct was located on the wall opposite the throne; about 100 feet.

The room was silent, he must wait. While going up he noticed that every so often square cubicles were carved on the sides of the duct, probably needed to carve the duct; there was one close to the exit point so he went down and sat on it – then waited.

******

Half an hour later – noises were heard; it was Uranus and he was calling for the usher that was waiting on the corridor in front of the Throne Room access door.

When the usher heard the ringing of the bell he entered the room and Uranus asked, "Are they here?"

"Yes, Your Excellency, they are," the usher answered.

"Good, let them in," Uranus said as he went over and sat on the throne.

Torr could hear everything from where he was sitting. The acoustics of the room were excellent. There was no reason for him to levitate to get closer.

The usher entered the room and announced the visitors; he said, "Your excellency, as summoned by you; Iltar, Esman, General Darko, and three of the higher ranking soldiers that witnessed what took place are present."

"Yes, yes, now go," Uranus told the usher; then to the others, "Now...all of you get closer."

The soldiers had never seen such opulence; once in front of the throne Uranus asked them, "Now...from the beginning; tell us what went on from the moment that you arrived at Mohenjo-Daro."

The three soldiers looked at each other; then the higher ranking one said, "We landed on schedule. At sunrise, somebody from the Citadel came over and General Khun and the ambassador accompanied him to the Citadel. When they came back groups were formed during the day so that we could visit the city. The cooks and soldiers went to the market and purchased among other things fresh fruits. The general and the officers also visited the city. That night General Khun, the ambassador, and the officers attended a banquet.

"In the morning the ambassador went to the Citadel and when he came back the squadrons were formed and told to march toward the Citadel, and that is when it happened; the officers and the ambassador fell to the ground – dead."

"That can't be, Uranus said. "You must have seen something. Was there a weapon fired; an arrow, a firearm or some kind of ray that you have never seen before?"

"Not that we could see," the soldier answered. "If it was a death ray we don't know about one that could do that, we don't have one."

Uranus then asked the other two soldiers, "What about the two of you; do you agree with what he is telling us?"

"Yes, we agree," the other two soldiers said. "That's exactly what took place."

Uranus asked, "Did the officers tell you why the troops were marching toward the Citadel?"

"No, we assumed that we were parading to show off our military capabilities," the higher ranking soldier answered and the other two assented.

Uranus then told the soldiers, "That's all I need to know...you can leave now and go back to your squadrons at the Air Base."

The others had been silent – when the soldiers left Uranus exploded, "Iltar!!! I remember you convincing me about a win-win situation. What do you have to say now?"

"Your Excellency, I can't explain, we'll try to find out the reason behind what took place," Iltar said.

"You better do, I don't buy this story about marching toward the Citadel." Uranus said; then looking at the general asked, "And what about you General Darko? You lost a general and three of your officers; not to mention that your forces were humiliated by an army that uses bows and arrows and depend on elephants to transport their soldiers."

"Your Excellency, I suggest that we retaliate; destroy their army and Mohenjo-Daro." General Darko suggested.

"Not so fast general, I must make sure that they were not up to something else and deserve their fate." Uranus said; then asked, "Or was there some other intentions that I have not been told?"

General Darko looked at Iltar, nodded in his direction and then said, "Your Excellency, I assure you that we were only trying to secure extra income for our treasury by offering protection and commercial treaties."

"We'll see about that," Uranus said; then looking at Esman said, "And you lost one of your ambassadors. Is there anything that you want to tell me, and that I should know?"

Esman answered, "Your Excellency, I was told to assign one of my ambassadors to the expedition so that he could negotiate the treaties; that's all I know."

General Darko insisted, "Your Excellency, "Are you going to do nothing? I suggest we send our vailxi (airships) and teach them a lesson."

Chronus exploded again, "No! No! No...First; we have to find out what killed our men and why it was done; then we'll decide what to do.

"Please leave now and the three of you better start looking as to why this had to happen."

Torr found out more than he expected. For one thing, the way General Darko reacted told him that he was one of the conspirators – wanted to destroy Mohenjo-Daro to cover up the failed extortion plot.

Of one thing Torr was sure, Uranus was not implicated.

As for Iltar, like the general, he must be involved in the extortion plot; he was the one that convinced Uranus to go ahead and try to sign other protection treaties.

The Chief Ambassador – maybe, or maybe not, when one of his ambassadors went to Mayax he stayed there only one day. It could be possible that the man called in sick that day and Esman never suspected where he was, but, it could be the other way around, Esman could be one of the conspirators and knew what the ambassador was doing there; if that was the case Torr had three suspects identified.

Torr decided to go back to the air base; anyway, he can't leave till next morning. He may learn something new. He did learn that Chief Ambassador Esman was present before the transports left, and that he talked with his ambassador and General Khun.

Torr remembered that the soldiers mentioned that all the officers and the ambassador had gone to a banquet the previous night; what happened there may have triggered the next day events.

The visit of the ambassador to the Citadel next morning looks like if he was delivering an ultimatum – then the soldiers started to march toward the Citadel.

Torr concluded that the thing to do was to go to Mohenjo-Daro and try to locate somebody that had been at the banquet; most likely a prosperous merchant.

The rest of the day Torr didn't learn anything new. He was eager to return to the base but there was no other thing to do but wait.

CHAPTER 23

Next morning, an hour after sunrise, Torr rented a chariot and was driven to the western waterway chariot rental agency located by the Outer Wall Ring Road.

As Torr approached the agency front desk the agent came out to meet him and asked, "What can we do for you?"

Torr answered, "I have a problem, I have to get to the logging camp today and return tomorrow by the middle of the afternoon – my ship sails with the afternoon tide. I just found out that the boat left more than an hour ago. Is there any way that a chariot can catch up with the boat?"

"No way," the agent said.

"It is important," Torr said. "It has to do with an inheritance. I have to deliver a scroll before I sail."

"There is a way," the agent said. "It is the only way that you can accomplish what you need to do."

"And what would that be?" Torr asked.

The agent explained, "If you rent a chariot – with a driver – you can go all the way to the logging camp. It is quite expensive, not to mention the punishing ride, but, there is no other way."

"Yes, I imagine that it would be expensive." Torr said.

The agent explained, "The driver will have to change the team of horses eight times on both directions, not only that, he must spend the night in one of the inns and then return tomorrow; that's why it is expensive.

"As a matter of fact, if you use the waterway boat to return tomorrow morning you will be back before the driver returns with the chariot; it's the only way that you can get back on time if you want to ship out with the afternoon tide. The waterway boat arrives just about midafternoon."

"That will have to be," Torr said; then asked, "But, how much is it going to cost me?"

The agent told him, and after haggling over the price, Torr finally accepted; paid the agent, then asked, "When can we leave?"

"Right now," the agent said; then called one of his drivers and explained what was required of him.

You could see that the driver was not thrilled by the assignment; the agent then told him, "I will inform your family that you will return tomorrow afternoon."

A chariot was made ready for the trip; spare parts were loaded so that the chariot can be repaired in case of a breakdown. The roundtrip was about 400 miles. This chariot had seats not only for the passenger but also for the driver; it was used for long distance trips.

A short time after they were on their way.

******

It was getting to be late in the afternoon, they were almost there.

When they reached the logging camp the driver left Torr at the camp entrance and headed back; he will spend the night in the last irrigation canal junction inn that they went by.

Torr waited until the chariot disappeared from sight and then walked in the opposite direction.

The sun was about to disappear over the horizon.

About two-and-a-half hours later he left the waterway road and entered the road leading to Ralh's farm. From then on he walked in partial darkness, clouds would cover the light of the moon; on-and-off.

The first thing that Ralh asked when Torr reached the farm was, "Well, did you find what you were looking for?"

"Yes I did, and I have to leave immediately, so let's go to the ship," Torr said.

They went down to the basement, entered the tunnel that ended up at the cave where the ship rested, Ralh opened the secret door that gave access to the cave and as soon as Torr was aboard the ship Ralh returned to the tunnel and turned the lights off.

Torr started the engine mercury boiling cycle, and once the ship was ready he activated the secret code and the door slid open – the ship emerged from its hibernation and like a scalded cat took to the air; went up and disappeared into the night sky. Once at cruising altitude Torr transmitted the usual signal – returning to base.

******

An hour later – about midmorning, Muror's time – Torr reached the base; Kalac was waiting for him when he landed; they went straight to Caleb's office.

Once seated Kalac asked, "Well...what else did you find out? Ralh called us yesterday and told us what happened at Mohenjo-Daro."

Torr then went on and told them what he heard while Uranus interrogated the ones responsible for the debacle at Mohenjo-Daro; then added, "I have to go to Mohenjo-Daro, it is the only way that we can find what took place at the banquet; also, the reason for the ambassador visit to the Citadel in the morning. Was it an ultimatum?"

"That's what it looks like, an ultimatum," Kalac said.

Torr added, "During Uranus interrogation I heard that they were also trying to secure new trade agreements; if that is the case; it is safe to say that the city prominent merchants were invited to the banquet; if I can talk to one of them he may tell me what went on during the banquet."

"We can help you in that respect," Kalac said; then explained, "We have a contact there; a Murovian merchant that handles some of the products that we export from Muror. He has a large store in the market square. I'm sure he was invited to the banquet. I suggest that you dress as a Murovian merchant, that way you will blend with the market environment."

"That will help me in finding out what I'm after," Torr said. "But, there is no place that we know where I can land and hide the ship at a reasonable distance from the city of Mohenjo-Daro."

Kalac then said, "That's no problem, I can drop you off close to the city before first light, and then pick you up after sundown."

Caleb added, "It looks like if we have a plan. Now...I must assume that you are leaving tomorrow. At what time are you leaving?"

Kalac did some calculations then told Torr, "We must leave at noon tomorrow."

Caleb then said, "Kalac will drop you off at the village, and pick you up tomorrow. You better go home and get some sleep, you need it.

"By the way, tonight; you are invited to dinner at my house. Be there an hour after sundown."

"I will be there," Torr said.

Kalac then said, "Let's go, I'll drop you off at the village. Tomorrow, I'll pick you up an hour before departure time."

They went over to the ship and left the base – Kalac dropped off Torr at the village and headed home.

As for Torr, it was going to be the first night that he would stay in his new home. The first thing he did before going to bed was to take a shower to get rid of the blond dye on his hair.

******

Torr slept for about six hours, now he must wait for the sun to disappear over the horizon.

After sundown he waited for an hour, and then headed for Caleb's house, he couldn't wait to see Lena again.

Caleb opened the front door; behind him stood his wife Omiga and his daughter Lena; they greeted Torr and escorted him to the dining room; a typical Murovian dining room – stone seats covered by a cushion of furs; and in front of each seat, stone blocks that served as a table.

After they took their seats the maid was summoned and food was served. While they partook of the earthly bounty they talked about their families. Lena wanted to know more about Torr's family. Torr told her that his father was a healer. Lena then mentioned that in one month (twenty days) she will become the village healer. The present healer will retire and move with his wife to Tuin where his offspring resides.

The conversation then shifted to the different leisure activities available to the residents of the village.

From then on Lena and Torr exchanged anecdotes about their school experiences.

It was getting late, the maid cleared the tables, and Torr decided that it was time to go; so, he told them, "I want to thank you for inviting me to dinner, but, it's getting late and I'm afraid I must leave. It has been a memorable evening."

"I'll let you out," Caleb said; and as he escorted Torr to the front door told him, "Make sure that you get plenty of sleep, tomorrow will be a long...long day for you."

"I know," Torr said; then returned to his new home.

******

Next day, about midmorning, Kalac stopped at the village to pick up Torr. Once at the base Torr changed into his new disguise – a Murovian merchant outfit.

Kalac then briefed Torr; gave him one of the portable beacon locators and told him, "When we find a good place to land I will fire a beacon into the ground, the locator is so that you can find the place at night. I will activate the beacon at sundown so that both of us can find the place." Then unfolding a map he had in his pocket said, "I'll show you the merchant's store location, take a look.

"If you enter the city from the south you will be on Main Street; that's where the market is located.

"As you head north count the streets on your left; after the first one the next exit to the left is a passage that connects to another parallel street on the western side of Main Street.

"Right in front of the passage entrance, on the opposite side of the street, to your right, you will see one of the few two story buildings on Main Street; that's where you can find our merchant."

It was getting to be time to leave. They checked the outside of the ship, went aboard, took off and headed in a northwest direction – next stop Mohenjo-Daro; one of the Rishi-Cities of the Naga Empire.

******

An hour went by – they overtook the arc of light, entered the dark zone, and a short time after, Mohenjo-Daro was seen on the horizon.

Once over the south side of the city Kalac started his search for a suitable place to land; he followed a trail that ran parallel to the river, and then they saw it; a small clearing between the trail and the river, and most important, it was surrounded by trees and there were no buildings in the vicinity.

Using the magnifying screen they made sure that the place was uninhabited. Then Kalac fired a beacon into the ground and told Torr, "When you leave the ship stay by the trees, behind the trees, until the sun rises over the horizon, and then head for the city; that way you will be able to recognize the road so you wouldn't get lost on your way back.

"An hour after sundown I will activate the beacon and wait for your signal. If it is safe to land use your portable beacon locator and turn it off and then back on, if it is not safe because there are people on the road then turn it off and on three times; if that is the case I will wait until you decide it is safe to pick you up."

Kalac then landed; dropped off Torr and headed for the base. He will be back in about twelve hours.

While waiting for the new dawn Torr realized why this land was uninhabited and was not used for farming; it was a flood field. The overflowing of the river would destroy anything planted on these fields.

Torr waited until the sun made its appearance over the horizon, and then headed for the city that was about four miles away.

It took Torr about two hours to reach Mohenjo-Daro.

The city was coming alive. The merchants were starting to set up their wares in front of their stores.

Torr went directly to where the passage was located, and there it was, as Kalac told him; in front of him the two story building.

Torr approached the store. A man was setting up the merchandise on a table in front of the store; Torr asked him, "Are you the owner?"

"Yes I am," the man said.

Torr then asked, "Are you from Muror?"

"Yes, and I see that you also are," the man said; then asked, "What can I do for you?"

"Muror's high officials would like to know what took place when the Atlanteans where here. Where you invited to the banquet?"

"Yes, I was invited," the man said.

"What happened during the banquet, anything out of the ordinary?" Torr asked.

The man answered, "The Atlanteans offered the king a Military Protection Treaty but he refused to consider such a treaty claiming that it was not needed because the nomad tribes would never dare to attack the villages located by the Western frontier. All the merchants present were for the treaty but the king was adamant.

"Next morning, right after sunrise, their ambassador was seen at the Citadel; when he returned to the landing site the troops started to march toward the Citadel. As the troop advanced the king stood atop the garrison tower; then, he raised his arms to heaven and we saw some of their men collapse; that stopped the march.

"They took the men that collapsed back to one of the transports, then the rest of the men returned to the ships, and not long after, the transports took off and disappeared over the Western horizon. Does that help?"

"Oh, yes," Torr said; then asked, "Are you sure that the men collapsed when the king raised his arms?"

"Yes, everybody saw it," the man answered.

Torr then asked, "Was there any weapons used against the marching troops?"

"Not that we saw or heard," the man said.

"You have been a great help and we thank you," Torr said, "I must leave now, take care."

Torr spent the rest of the time reconnoitering the city and about midafternoon headed for the pickup point; once there he waited by the trees for more than an hour after sundown, then he looked both ways down the road; all was clear and he turned the beacon on and off.

Within a very short time Torr saw the ship materialize not far from where he was standing; he ran over and climbed aboard, and not long after, the ship darted upward vanishing from view. They were on their way back to the base.

Once at cruising altitude Kalac asked, "Well, did you find our man?"

"Yes I did," Torr answered; then added, "He attended the banquet, and he corroborated what we suspected; they were trying to sell protection treaties, but the Rishi-King refused the offer. It is possible that the ambassador was delivering an ultimatum when he went to the Citadel next morning. The rest of the story coincides with what I heard from the soldiers when they were interrogated by Uranus.

"One thing that I can't figure out is how they managed to kill their officers and the ambassador."

Kalac said, "We think we know. The Rishi-King is a Grand Master capable of controlling matter; including a person heartbeat. Tomorrow at the meeting we'll talk some more about what we think is happening."

******

An hour later they landed at the base, it was past midnight. Torr stayed at the base and Kalac went home; he will be back by midmorning.

CHAPTER 24

Back at Semira – Esman was asking Iltar, "What are we going to do? With Khun dead we lost our contact with the mechanic that is going to sabotage Chronus' ship; we are lucky that Khun gave us his name before he left for Mohenjo-Daro. The mechanic was told to go ahead with the plan no matter what, that other officials knew who he was, and that he will get paid as promised."

Iltar said, "Then, all we have to do is to reassure him that he can proceed as planned, and that he will get paid."

"But, there is a problem," Esman said.

"What do you mean?" Iltar asked.

"We don't have a boat," Esman said.

"What! Oh...I see; the loose end," Iltar said. "It means that we can't let him know who we are."

Esman then said, "There is no need for us to meet him face to face, he knows what has to be done, and that he will get paid."

Iltar suggested, "All we have to do is to find out where he lives, and while he is at work slide a folded and sealed scroll under his front door. The message only has to read; 'The agreement is still good, you can proceed'. He will understand."

Esman then asked, "It sounds good, but how do we find out where he lives?"

After a short moment of silence Iltar said, "We were ordered by Uranus to investigate, to get to the bottom of what happened. You lost one of your ambassadors and you are supposed to participate in the search for any clues that could clarify the reasons behind the actions of the officers and the ambassador.

"So, you can show up at Khun's office and tell the office clerk that you have been ordered by Uranus to investigate Khun's death, and that you need to check his office and files. While at the office check the military personnel files, you should find the address there."

"Yes, it should work," Esman said. "I'm leaving right now for the base, I'll report to you as soon as I get back."

"Another thing," Iltar said. "As soon as you find out his address write the message, and on your way back deliver the scroll to his home before you return to the palace.

"And very important, make sure that you are not seen while sliding the scroll under the door."

Esman then left the palace and headed for the air base.

******

Upon reaching General Khun's office Esman gained access to the general military personnel files. It didn't take long to find what he was looking for. Then he wrote the note for the mechanic and went back to the city, found the mechanic's home, slid the note under the front door, and then headed back for the palace.

******

When Esman entered Iltar's office he found General Darko there; they were waiting for him.

Now, it would be expected that the three of them be seen holding meetings; everybody in the palace knew that Uranus had assigned them to find out the reason behind the debacle at Mohenjo-Daro.

Once Esman sat down Iltar asked, "Does any of you have any idea as to what we are going to do? We have to assume that the Rishi-King didn't accept our proposal and they were trying to get rid of the present king."

"That's what most likely happened," Darko said.

"We have a big problem in our hands," Esman said.

"Yes indeed," Darko said. "I suggest, like I said before, that we send a squadron of vailxi and obliterate their city; that way the other kingdoms will not dare refuse our offer."

"Hold it there, we can't do that without justifying our actions to Uranus," Esman said; then suggested, "Let's wait a few days before we report back to Uranus, we have to build up our case. I suggest that we send a vailx to reconnoiter the city, and then tell Uranus that we landed a man close to the city. That the man spent three days in the city inquiring as to what took place and was able to talk to a merchant that attended the banquet; who told him that the king refused to sign a protection treaty and cancelled the active commercial treaty.

"That the man was able to confirm what the soldiers told us and worse yet – the talk of the town was that they could have killed the rest of the soldiers if they wanted, and killing our leaders was a sample of what they could do. That they were laughing at us.

"We can also tell Uranus that if we don't do anything the other kingdoms that have protection treaties with us could cancel the treaties – we'll be humiliated, and a lot of revenue lost."

"That may convince Uranus, it sounds like a good excuse to eradicate their city from the face of the planet," Iltar said; adding, "We can't let them get away with it."

General Darko then said, "I see that the two of you finally agree with me as to what has to be done. If we can convince Uranus with that story and he gives the go ahead I guarantee that next day, the city of Mohenjo-Daro will be erased from the surface of the planet.

"Tonight I'll send a vailx to reconnoiter Mohenjo-Daro. I'll time the departure so that he will arrive over the city in the early morning, their time. Three days later the ship will go back and do the same; that would legitimize our story with Uranus."

Esman asked, "What if Uranus wants to interrogate the man that supposedly went to Mohenjo-Daro? Uranus may be old but he is no fool."

For some time there was total silence, then Darko said, "It will have to be me, I need to disappear for three days and I know how to do it without raising any suspicions, and if Uranus were to ask; our story can be corroborated."

"What do you mean by disappear?" Iltar asked.

Darko answered, "I have a relative that has a farm near Trell; the pilot can drop me off on his farm and pick me up three days later when he returns from Mohenjo-Daro. The flight line personnel will see me going on the first trip and returning on the second trip three days later."

"But, what about the pilot," Iltar asked.

"That's no problem," Darko said. "I've known him for a long time, he can keep a secret. I'll tell him that I need some time by myself to plot the strategy to be used if we are ordered to attack Mohenjo-Daro. And to make it credible I'll tell him to update the map of the city; to look for any defensive forts not shown, or any other changes since our map was created, and then to bring me the map on his way back. I'll tell him to pick me up on his way back from his second trip three days later.

"He will be sworn to secrecy as to where I was, he will never suspect anything since I will tell him that I didn't want any interruptions; an impossibility in my office, and that I have to create different scenarios; from total annihilation to surgical strikes focused on the military garrisons so that Uranus can select what he thinks is the appropriate response; hence the need not to be disturbed, for I have a lot to consider."

Having reached an agreement Darko left the palace; went home to pack a change of clothes, and then headed for the Air Base to arrange for the night flight.

******

That night, about midnight, the pilot with Darko aboard left the Air Base. Once over Trell they located the farm, landed, and as Darko was leaving the ship he told the pilot, "You'll be back in less than three hours, I'll be waiting for you with the updated map."

"It will be done," the pilot said; then disappeared into the starred sky.

CHAPTER 25

It was midmorning at the Muror base – When Kalac arrived at the base he met Torr who had been waiting for him; both of them went straight to Caleb's office. As soon as they entered the office Caleb asked Torr, "Were you able to contact our man?"

"Yes I did," Torr answered. "He was invited to the banquet, and according to him they were trying to procure a Military Protection Treaty, but the Rishi-King refused to consider signing such a treaty; it wasn't needed according to him. The rest we already know; except for how the officers and the ambassador died."

Kalac then said, "We have an idea; we know that the only ones that die were the ones that attended the banquet, and that to be able to control matter you have to visualize what you want to control – that's why the only ones that were killed were the ones that attended the banquet; the king, a Grand Master; can stop anybody heartbeat if he can visualize that person face; and that is what probably happened in this case."

"Resuming what we know," Caleb said. "It is reasonable to surmise that a few of Uranus' high officials are involved in an extortion plot. Iltar is most likely calling the shots and the two generals and all the officers of the Assault Forces are the other conspirators. As for Esman we don't have definite proof – yet; but he is probably one of them."

Kalac added, "I suspect that if Iltar is the one that is behind all this there is an ulterior motive behind, the extortion plot is just a smoke screen; he needs the generals and the officers on his side when he takes over."

"What do you mean by take over?" Caleb asked.

"It is well known that Uranus is exhibiting signs of senility," Kalac said. "If Chronus were to die – in an accident – Iltar being the High-Priest would inherit the throne when Uranus dies or is incapacitated; if that was to happen Iltar needs the two generals in charge of the Assault Forces, the officers, and the ambassadors on his side; hence the plot to make them rich before he becomes the king."

"We have a situation; a bad one if I may say," Caleb said. "Iltar must be planning on killing Chronus, probably in an accident like Kalac says."

"So, what's our next move," Torr asked.

Kalac answered, "I'll have to report all we know to the Archpriest. Also, let's call Ralh and see if in the next two days any military expeditions leave Semira; and if so, try to find out their destination. It will take him three days to be back from Semira, there is a two day travel time plus the day he will stay in Semira."

"Who will tell Uranus?" Caleb asked.

Kalac answered, "Once Ralh reports what he has learned I'll go to Semira as an envoy from the Archpriest and request an audience with Uranus. We can't send an ambassador so it will have to be me. The Atlanteans know me and that I'm an advisor to the Archpriest.

"Let's wait three days to see what Ralh reports, and then I'll have one of the Archpriest pilots take me to Semira in one of the civilian ships."

Torr asked, "Meanwhile, what can I do?"

Kalac answered, "Well, I tell you what, I'll drop you off at the village on my way to Nalta. There may be things that you have to purchase for the house, and as I remember you need to hire a housekeeper.

"During the three days spend some time at the base and study the weaponry installed in the antigravity ship. Take the ship out over the ocean and fire the weapons as many times as you need so you become familiar with their range capabilities, and also practice abrupt defensive maneuvers. Remember, that ship is faster than your ship."

Caleb opened a drawer; there was a code transmitter inside, and then proceeded to send a message to Ralh telling him what he wanted done.

After that was done Kalac told Torr, "I'm leaving for Nalta; I'll drop you off at the village on my way there. So, let's go."

They left the base, and after leaving Torr at the village Kalac headed for Nalta.

******

Torr went directly to his new home; it was empty; a fortress of solitude; and then an image intruded upon his mind – Lena.

Torr remembered that Lena was supposed to be working at the village clinic so he headed that way; hopping that she was there; she was. As soon as he entered the clinic he saw her; she smiled at him and said, "I wasn't expecting you, I thought that the last few days you were in Nalta, working for the Archpriest."

"The Archpriest!!! Oh...yes. Well, I'm back, and will be trying to hire a housekeeper to take care of my house. As I remember your mother offered to help me find one."

"Yes she did," Lena said. "She told you the first time we met; at the boat dock."

Torr then said, "It's getting to be lunch time, would you consider having lunch with me?"

"Not only would I love to, but I will invite you to come over to my house and have lunch with me. As you know the scribes eat at the temple.

Our maid cooks my lunch but she has the day off, she is visiting a sick relative. So, I'll prepare something for the two of us."

"Does that mean that you know how to cook?" Torr asked.

Both of them laughed at what was insinuated.

******

As soon as Kalac landed at the Nalta temple he was ushered to the Archpriest office. The moment he entered the office the Archpriest asked him, "Well...can you tell me what is going on? Do you know or suspect who is behind what is happening?"

Kalac told the Archpriest everything they knew so far.

"Then, what are you planning on doing?" the Archpriest asked; then added, "We have to be sure before we act."

Kalac answered, "I'm planning on going to Semira in three days and have a talk with Uranus, we have to inform him of what some of his officials are doing and what we suspect is their final intention with regard to the throne."

"How about sending an ambassador? The Archpriest asked.

"No way," Kalac answered; then added, "If we use an ambassador we'll have to tell him how we gathered the facts, and that would imply the use of a covert operator – a warrior priest. We can't jeopardize future operations.

"I need one of our civilian ships, and one of your pilots to take me there."

"Anything you need," the Archpriest said. "Before you leave today, inform the pilot so that he will be ready.

"I'll send a message to Uranus to expect your visit."

"When I return you will be the first to know the outcome of my visit," Kalac said.

"So be it," the Archpriest said. "If there is nothing else; the Gods be with you," and after he said that left the room.

Kalac went down to the hangar; there he talked to the pilot and arranged for the use of the ship; that done he headed back home.

CHAPTER 26

At the secret outpost in Poseidia – Ralh received a coded message; 'Go to Semira, go to the air base and look for any unusual activity with regard to the Assault Forces and the vailxi fighters. Stay there one day, return and report any deployments'.

Next day Ralh left the farm and by midafternoon reached Semira. The first thing he did was to secure a room at the inn; left there the bag he was carrying, then went over to a funicular station and headed for the air base.

At the air base – he asked around, the Assault Forces had not left the base, neither the vailxi fighters.

Ralh returned to Semira and spent the rest of the afternoon listening to the latest gossip; there was nothing new. He will try again tomorrow.
******

Next morning at the palace – Iltar and Esman were in the presence of Uranus who wanted to know if they had anything new to report, so Uranus asked, "Now...the two of you...by the way, where is General Darko? And did you find anything new that I don't know?"

"Your Excellency," Iltar answered. "We have a man in Mohenjo-Daro; he is trying to contact somebody that may have attended the banquet; he will be back tomorrow."

"I want to talk to him the morning after his return," Uranus said; then asked, "What about the general?"

"Your excellency, he is at work, and will be here the next time we report," Iltar said.

Uranus then said, "If there is nothing new to report you can leave now."

As they came out of the Throne Room Esman remarked, "Uranus acted as we suspected that he would, he wants to talk to the man that went to Mohenjo-Daro."

Iltar added, "That's why it is so important to be one step ahead."

Then they returned to their respective offices in the palace.
******

That same morning – while Uranus was meeting with Iltar and Esman – Ralh was back at the air base; there were no visible changes, no indication of any deployment of troops, or that the vailxi had left the base.

Ralh returned to the city and spent the rest of the day listening to what the people at the market were saying about the Mohenjo-Daro incident, and there was nothing new. He will be back home tomorrow afternoon and will transmit a message informing that there was nothing out of the ordinary going on at the air base.

******

That same night – at midnight – General Darko returned to Semira.

******

In the morning – while Ralh was on a boat heading home, General Darko, Iltar and Esman were waiting to be admitted to the Throne Room.

The usher showed up and told them; "Please, follow me." then opened the door to the room and led them to the throne where Uranus waited.

They stood now in front of Uranus who stared at then and said, "I see three of you. Where is the man that went to Mohenjo-Daro?"

"Your Excellency," General Darko said. "I was the one that went there."

"What are you talking about?" Uranus questioned.

"Your Excellency," Darko explained. "It was a covert operation; we don't want others to know what we may be planning on doing.

"Also, I needed to reconnoiter their military defense installations, in case you elect to order a military strike. As you can see I was the indicated one to go."

"Yes, but you risked your life, and that's not what we need now, the loss of another general," Uranus said; then asked, "Why I wasn't told?"

"Your Excellency," Iltar said. "We didn't want you to worry."

"Well...what is done is done," Uranus said. "Now, what do you have to tell us that we don't know?"

General Darko started to tell Uranus the story they had concocted, and when he mentioned that they were laughing at them Uranus blew a gasket; he stood up and said, "Laughing at us!!! I'll show them."

Esman then added, "Your Excellency, not only are they laughing at us, but if we don't teach them a lesson other kingdoms that have a Military Protection Treaty with us will most likely cancel their treaty. And we know what that means; a loss of revenue."

General Darko asked, "Your Excellency, what do you want us to do?"

Uranus then asked the general, "Do you have any ideas as to the possible retaliation alternatives?"

"Your Excellency," Darko answered. "Yes I have, and I have with me the plans for the possible alternatives."

Uranus thought about it, hesitated, and then told the general, "Leave your alternative plans with me and be back this afternoon; then, I'll tell you which alternative I have selected. Now, go back to your offices."

When they left the room Iltar said, "Let's meet in my office, we have to plan how to proceed."

Once in Iltar's office they sat around a table; General Darko then laid a map of Mohenjo-Daro on the table; the three of them looked at it, then,

General Darko said, "The way I see it, no matter what Uranus decides, there will be some collateral damage. If we obliterate everything, Uranus would not suspect anything if we tell him that our weapons are too powerful and we could not avoid the damage to the rest of the city. I suspect that he will order us to destroy only the military garrisons."

Iltar then said, "Talking about military garrisons, there is a large one near Harappa, how about destroying it, and of course, the village of Harappa."

Esman asked, "If the garrison is not in the village, how are we going to account for the destruction of the village?"

"That's easy," Darko explained. "We'll tell Uranus that when I flew over the village on my way to check on the garrison I was intercepted by a military vimana that we never suspected they had, and that during the air battle that ensued some of the shots that were fired – and missed the target – ended up hitting the village of Harappa and the garrison. Uranus will be told that we split our forces; three of the vailxi were to attack Mohenjo-Daro and the other was only supposed to reconnoiter the Harappa garrison and the village – to update our maps.

"I will lead the mission, and will attack Harappa. The three officers will pilot the other three vailxi – one on each, no other crewmembers."

"Well...we seem to be one step ahead, so let's wait to see what Uranus decides this afternoon," Iltar said.

******

That same morning some maintenance work was being done at the hangar that houses the ships used by Uranus and Chronus. It seems that they needed to access an underground tunnel to replace some electrical wires. The access to the tunnel was right under where Uranus park his vailx; so they moved his ship to the empty spot used by Chronus.

******

That same day – by midafternoon Ralh was back at his farm. A message was transmitted to Muror; 'No activity at the base'.

Kalac was informed. He calculated his departure time so he would arrive at the Royal Palace by dawn, next day.

******

Late that afternoon General Darko returned to the Royal Palace to find out what Uranus had decided to do.

As Darko approached the throne he asked Uranus, "Your Excellency, what do you want us to do?"

"I have studied your alternative plans and I have decided to destroy their military installations – their garrisons."

"Your Excellency, I should mention that there is going to be collateral damage; their garrisons are too close to the civilian population; one is in

137

the Citadel and the other is by the river and the north side of the city wall."

"If that is the way it has to be...it will have to be," Uranus said; then asked, "By the way, how many vailxi are you sending?"

"Your Excellency, there will be four, and I will pilot one of them. I'm planning on leading the operation."

"Hmm...I see," Uranus said. "And I must assume...that there would be no losses this time?"

"Not this time Your Excellency, this time we are not landing, and they don't have any ships that can oppose our ships. There is nothing to worry about." Darko explained.

Uranus then said, "I want you to plan an attack for tomorrow. If you leave an hour before midmorning, our time, you can reach your target by midafternoon – their time.

"You can go now, get the ships ready, and report to me as soon as you get back."

General Darko left the room and headed for Iltar's office, where Iltar and Esman waited.

As soon as the general walked into the room Iltar asked, "Well...are we going? And what alternative did he select?"

Darko answered, "He selected the military installations as I suspected he would."

"That means," Iltar said, "that we can go ahead with what we were planning on doing."

"The three officers and I will pilot the four ships, no need for other crewmembers." Darko said.

General Darko and the other three officers were capable of flying the ships. Any officer assigned to the Assault Forces was trained as a pilot.

The general went over to the air base; held a meeting with the officers and told them what they were planning on doing, how it was going to be accomplished and what they would tell Uranus when they get back.

After the meeting the general went over to the flight line and requested that four vailxi – with full armament, be ready to fly – next morning – by sunrise.

******

That same afternoon Chronus had made plans to return to Semira next day. He was planning on getting there in the early morning.

The news of what happened to the Assault Forces when they visited Mohenjo-Daro had reached Sais the day after it happened. A message was received from Semira – Sais was an Atlantis colony and had to be advised about the possible repercussions; in their case trade issues.

After the initial message nothing was heard for the next three days; that's why Chronus decided that it was time to return to Semira.

CHAPTER 27

Next morning – in Semira, while the general and the three officers were at the air base getting their vailxi ready..., at Nalta; Kalac was about to leave for Semira; and so Chronus from Sais. Both of them will converge in Semira sometime after sunrise, Semira time.

******

Muror time – midnight. Kalac and the Archpriest pilot left the Great Temple underground cave and were now flying eastward. It will take about an hour to reach Semira.

As they approached Poseidia the sun made its appearance over the Eastern horizon. Once over their territory a call was placed to the Semira Air Base control tower requesting permission to land at the visitors' landing pad by the Royal Palace. Permission was granted, they had been advised by the Archpriest that they were coming.

The Archpriest pilot had been there before so he knew about the visitors' landing pad location – by the palace.

Kalac must wait about two hours before he could see Uranus; he will wait in the visitors' lounge.

******

While Kalac was waiting in the lounge for an audience with Uranus... – Chronus was about to park his vailx in his assigned landing pad, but there was a problem; the other palace vailx was occupying his landing pad.

Chronus landed in front of the hangar, located the crew chief; found him, and asked, "What is going on? How come the other vailx is on the wrong side?"

"Oh...don't worry," the crew chief said. "We had to access the wiring tunnel that runs under the hangar. The palace pilot is off today, so park on the number one pad; I'll tell him to switch them around tomorrow morning."

The problem solved, Chronus walked over to the funicular station and headed for the city of Semira; from there, using a chariot, he went straight to the palace.

Once at the palace Chronus went up to the third floor where the royal quarters were located and asked one of the servants, "Have you seen my Father today?"

Uranus private quarters, and also the Throne Room, are located on the fourth floor.

"Yes," the servant answered. "He came down and had breakfast earlier, and I believe that he is getting ready to receive an envoy from the Archpriest of Muror."

"An envoy from Muror!!!" Chronus exclaimed; then asked, "Do you have an idea as to where he is?"

The servant answered, "I was told that he is at the visitors' lounge."

Chronus then headed for the visitors' lounge but before he could get there he was approached by Amelius who had been looking for him after hearing that he was back.

They exchanged greetings, and then Amelius said, "It is important that I talk to you about something I overheard and may have something to do with the Mohenjo-Daro incident."

"Follow me," Chronus said. "Let me first find out why is an envoy from Muror here."

They went over to the visitors' lounge, and Amelius was told to wait outside.

Chronus went into the room and was surprised to see Kalac instead of an ambassador; they knew each other, so Chronus asked, "Kalac; my friend, what is so important that you are here instead of an ambassador?"

"It has to do with the Mohenjo-Daro incident, and that your life may be in danger." Kalac answered.

"What are you talking about?" Chronus asked.

"Uranus is getting older, and as you must know, he is delegating some of his authority to Iltar and to the military. Well...they are taking advantage of him. We have uncovered a plot to extract unauthorized payments not called for in your military treaties. We are assuming that Iltar is the one orchestrating the plot for he is the one with the most to gain as I will explain when we talk with Uranus."

Chronus then said, "I just arrived from Sais and was informed by one of my servants that an envoy from Muror was waiting to have an audience with my Father, that's why I came down to see what all this is about. On my way to the lounge I met with Amelius – our royal scribe – who also wants to talk to me about the same subject; he is waiting outside, so let's join him and go see Uranus."

They went up to the fourth floor and Chronus told the usher that they needed to talk to Uranus, as soon as possible.

A short time after, the usher returned and told them, "All of you can go in," and then opened the door for them.

They went in – seeing the three of them together Uranus said, "What an odd coalition – Chronus, Kalac, and Amelius," then looking at Chronus said, "I just found out that you were back, will you please tell me why the three of you are here?"

Chronus then answered, "I'll let Amelius and Kalac tell you what they know for I don't know the whole story."

Amelius then told Uranus, "While I was looking for some old scrolls stored in the basement I overheard some of the kingdom officials that were plotting to extort extra compensation not called for in our Military Protection Treaties."

Kalac then said, "He is telling the truth. We found out that they are already extorting the Kingdom of Mayax." then looking at Amelius asked, "How come you didn't tell Uranus?"

Amelius answered, "Because of the people involved in the plot I thought that Uranus may not believe me; and if that was the case, my life would had been in danger, I would be dead by now – died in an accident, of course."

Uranus ordered, "Tell us their names."

"Iltar seemed to be their leader, I recognized his voice," Amelius answered, "but I couldn't recognize the other voices. One was addressed as a general and the others were most likely the officers under his command."

"As for what happened at Mohenjo-Daro, we know for a fact," Kalac then added, "that the Rishi-King refused to sign a protection treaty; hence the march toward the Citadel in the morning; most likely, it was with the intention of doing away with the present king."

Chronus asked Kalac, "You told me that my life was in danger; why?"

Kalac answered, "We have concluded that the extortion plot is a smoke screen. Iltar is the High-Priest, and if you happen to be dead he would inherit the throne when Uranus dies. Right now, they must be planning your accident.

"If Iltar was to claim the throne he needs the officers of the Assault Forces to back him up – hence the extortion plots to make them rich."

"If what you found out is true," Uranus said, "then we have to assume that the two generals and the six officers assigned to the Assault Forces are Iltar's co-conspirators."

"Yes, it looks that way," Kalac said.

Then Uranus remembered, "Esman...what about Esman? He must be one of them; there is no way that he doesn't know what his ambassadors are doing."

"Maybe..., or maybe not," Kalac said. "The same way they deceived you in the acquisition of more protection treaties they could have done the same to him. He may claim that he was ordered to provide an ambassador to negotiate the treaties, and to also help them convince you that it was a good idea to try to generate more income for the kingdom. Now...the ambassador that went on the mission had to know, unfortunately, he is dead; so there is no way to find out if he was following Esman orders regarding the extortion or if he was acting on his own."

"I have been deceived," Uranus said. "They convinced me that we have to retaliate. Right now they must be about to take off from the air base. I have approved the destruction of the Mohenjo-Daro garrisons."

"You did what!!!" Chronus exclaimed; then asked, "How many vailxi are they sending?"

"Four, as I was told," Uranus said. "General Darko is leading the flight, and this morning I found out that three of his officers will be flying the other three ships. Who knows what they may be planning on doing?"

Kalac asked, "Can you stop them?"

"Not if they are already airborne," Chronus said. "Once the vailxi leave on a mission – according to the standard operating procedures – their transmitters and receivers are turned off; that's to make sure the enemy is not alerted."

******

Meanwhile; at the Air Base – General Darko was about to go aboard the ship that he will be flying, and before doing so told Iltar, "We'll be back in about three hours. If you want, you can wait for us in the civilian terminal."

Iltar decided to go to the civilian terminal and wait there, no use going back to his office at the palace and then having to turn around after a short wait.

******

Uranus rang a bell, the usher showed up; Uranus then told him, "Go down to the communications station and tell the priest there to call the air base, and to request that they check to see if the four vailxi are still there; if they are; they are to be told to abort the mission."

Chronus asked his Father, "Do you happen to know where Iltar and Esman can be found?"

"They should be at their offices here in the palace," Uranus answered.

"Let me go get them," Chronus said; then went down to the first floor, stopped at the palace guard offices and requested that a guard accompany him. He will arrest Iltar when he finds him.

Iltar was not in his office and his assistant didn't know where he was. Chronus found Esman in his office and told him, "Follow me, Uranus wants to talk to you."

Chronus dismissed the palace guard; he wouldn't need him, for now.

Chronus returned with Esman to the Throne Room; when they entered the room the first thing that Uranus asked Chronus was, "Where is Iltar?"

"Not to be found," Chronus answered.

Uranus queried Esman, "One of your ambassadors is dead. Do you know or suspect what he was up to?"

"Your excellency, what are you talking about? All I know is that General Khun needed an ambassador to negotiate Military Protection Treaties, and Iltar and Khun suggested that I should help them convince you that it was a great idea; that it would mean extra income for our treasury. They even told me which one of the ambassadors they wanted."

"Probably the same one that went to Mayax," Kalac said.

Uranus then told Esman, "Go back to your office."

Esman had just left the room when the usher returned; he told Uranus, "Your Excellency, the vailxi were taking off when the priest placed the call to the air base, and as you know there is no way to contact them."

When Kalac heard that he told Uranus, "I have done what I came to do. Since there is nothing else that I can do, I'm afraid that I have to return to Muror."

"So be it and we thank you," Uranus said.

Kalac went back to his airship. They left Semira and when they reached cruising altitude Kalac transmitted a coded message to the priest monitoring the base control room. A priest was always monitoring the screens on the base control room – day and night. To the villagers or any outsider, the priest that stayed behind during the night was there to guard the temple scrolls.

The priest at the control room deciphered the message, it read; 'Call Torr and tell him that this is an emergency, and that he must go to the landing pad as soon as possible. That you will pick him up, and that once at the base he must take the anti-gravity ship out and head west flying at maximum speed, then to contact Kalac once he is airborne'. The rest of the message read; 'Because of the urgency, you must leave the base, land at the village landing pad and pick up Torr. As you know, you are not supposed to be seen flying an airship. Make sure that you are not seen in the cockpit. It is still dark. Don't turn the lights on in the cockpit when you land'.

All the priests that worked at the secret base were capable of flying the airships, even if they were not the Priest-Scientists.

There was a direct line from the control room to the homes of the priests that worked at the base. The priest called Torr and gave him Kalac's message. Then he positioned a lever that will allow him to open the door when he returns to the base; after having done that he went down to the hangar, and a short time after was on his way to the village to pick up Torr.

When the priest reached the village Torr was already waiting by the landing pad.

They returned to the base; once there Torr went directly to the ship, left the base, and using the maximum speed capabilities of the ship headed west.

As instructed Torr contacted Kalac who sent a coded message back. Torr decoded the message; it read, 'Seek, intercept, and destroy four vailxi from Atlantis that are heading for Mohenjo-Daro with the intention of destroying the city. Destroy them no matter what'.

******

Esman didn't return to his office and headed for the air base, he knew that Iltar had gone there to check with the general if there had been any changes to their plan of attack. Iltar for sure must be planning to wait for their return. And because its facilities; the civilian terminal was the only reasonable place to wait.

As he predicted, Esman found Iltar at the terminal.

Iltar was surprised to see Esman so he asked, "What are you doing here?"

Esman answered, "I came to warn you, Uranus knows about our extortion plot, they know about you, the general, and the officers. The palace guards have been ordered to arrest you – on sight. They can't prove anything against me – yet, but when the officers get back they will be arrested and submitted to brain scans, then, they will know about me.

"As long as they don't arrest any of the officers I'll be able to help in whatever we decide to do. I'm going over to the military side of the base and wait for their return so that I can warn the general and the officers of what is happening. I'll bring them here.

"Meanwhile you must hide here, but you have to get rid of your tunic. There is a clothing store in the housing suburb by the base gate, that's where most of the people that work here live. I'll go over and buy five civilian outfits; you can wear one, and when the general and the officers return they can use the other four disguises."

Esman then left the base, purchased the needed clothing and then returned to the base. Esman gave the package to Iltar and before he left for the military side of the base told him, "I almost forgot to tell you, Chronus is back; he arrived this morning. He knows about the plot."

Iltar said, "That means that our mechanic will work on his ship tonight; that may be what could save us if we have to make a run for it."

"What do you mean," Esman asked.

Iltar answered, "If tomorrow we were to steal Uranus vailx; who do you think will chase us? Chronus ship will blow up after flying for about half-an-hour."

Esman said, "With Chronus gone, and if the officers escape, it will be easy for me to control Uranus. But, meanwhile, you better start planning where to head for that would take more than half-an-hour of flying time."

Esman then left the civilian terminal and headed for the military terminal of the air base.

******

The mechanic that will sabotage Chronus vailx went to get some parts from the civilian parts stock room, and there they were; two vailxi side by side, Chronus was back – that meant that tonight he will be busy.

******

Kalac made it back to the base, and then went home.

CHAPTER 28

The four vailxi, with General Darko and the other three officers at the controls were now hovering over the city of Mohenjo-Daro. Scattered clouds covered the city and the surrounding fields.

General Darko's vailx left the formation and headed for Harappa, due north. The other three vailxi must wait until Darko was over his target; they had planned a simultaneous strike.

They positioned their vailxi over their aim points; the Citadel and the city, and then climbed to a safe altitude to wait for the order to fire their weapons.

On the outskirts of the city – farmers plowed their fields, animals leisurely grazed on the fields, and the birds sang what would be their last songs.

A few elephants were seen by the river piling what appeared to be logs that had been floated downstream.

It was time – word came from Darko; he was ready.

The stage was set. The three vailxi synchronized their firing, and like dragons belched what looked like bolts of lightning.

Flashes of light struck their targets – everything in sight melted, the sandy ground turned into glass, and an enormous cloud resembling a mushroom covered what used to be the city of Mohenjo-Daro.

The people on the outskirts of the city saw a flash of lightning hitting the city, and an instant later the wave generated by the blast flattened the countryside. Anything close to the city was on fire or dying. Even the elephants that where by the river were affected, they jumped into the river; their skins seared by the intense heat generated by the blast. Dead birds were falling from the sky.

A similar situation was taking place in Harappa.

After firing their weapons the three vailxi had flown on a western direction to a rendezvous point where they waited for General Darko to join them; once that happened they headed for Semira.

******

Before he could see Mohenjo-Daro Torr knew that he didn't get there on time; huge clouds could be seen on the horizon. Torr was horrified when he came within sight of Mohenjo-Daro; clouds still covered the city, and a few miles away dead animals and people covered the adjacent fields.

It was evident that this had just happened so their ships should be close by, and on their way back to Semira.

His ship was much faster so Torr climbed to a higher altitude and headed in the general direction of Semira hopping to see the trails left by the vailxi; he was ordered to destroy them, no matter what.

Not after he overflew Sais did he saw what he was looking for; four white vapor trails framed against the blue background of the Inland Sea.

Torr overtook the vailxi, raced ahead, went down to their same flight level, reversed direction, and then in a hovering position faced them.

The Atlanteans started to fire from far away when they saw Torr's ship but Torr had foreseen what they would do and an instant before they fired their weapons he had made his ship jump to a higher altitude; their shots missed. The light beams passed underneath Torr's ship. Torr then aligned his sight on one of the vailxi and then pressed the firing button; held it for a short time and the vailx blew up. Pieces of what once was a vailx were now falling down from the sky and sinking into the ocean.

The other three vailxi went by underneath Torr's ship and reversing their heading returned to engage him.

The pilots of the three remaining vailxi were amazed, they never saw a light beam hit the vailx that blew up.

The vailxi weapons leave a light trail – from weapon to target.

The weapon that Torr used was a secret technology unknown to the Atlanteans. A powerful invisible pulse sent to the target reads the molecular frequency of the intended material to be destroyed. Then, a highly amplified frequency of the molecular composition is sent back to the target and the object is disintegrated.

After the first kill a fierce battle ensued, but they were no match for Torr's ship; his ship was faster and had a faster response time with regard to positional changes.

One by one Torr obliterated the vailxi; when that was done he flew back to Mohenjo-Daro and then headed north, he had seen another mushroom cloud in that direction when he gained altitude to pursue the vailxi.

When Torr reached Harappa he was saddened by what he saw; they had destroyed two cities and he never had a chance to intercept them before they reached their targets.

There was nothing that Torr could do now. Using a slower speed he flew eastward, he didn't want to get back to the base before the beginning of the priests workday.

******

Meanwhile at the Semira Air Base, Esman and Iltar waited for General Darko and the officers to return from their mission. While Iltar waited in the civilian terminal Esman waited outside the entrance to the military terminal. He will wait outside the gate for he didn't want to be seen talking with the officers when they get back.

******

Torr was now heading back, and expected to be back at the base by the start of the new work day.

Below his flight path; total darkness. The darkness below contrasted with the starred sky; an amazing view from his altitude.

As soon as Torr landed he was told to report to Caleb's office where Caleb and Kalac were to debrief him.

Once in the office Torr told them how he had destroyed the four vailxi when they were returning to Semira, and that he felt sorry that he wasn't able to get there on time to prevent the destruction of Mohenjo-Daro and Harappa.

Kalac then said, "It is not our or your fault, there was not enough time, but at least, you did get rid of the perpetrators of the plot."

"What do you mean?" Torr asked.

Kalac answered, "General Darko and the other three officers from the Assault Forces were the ones flying the vailxi, and so, as you can see, you eliminated the remaining military members of the plot. When I left Semira the palace guards were trying to locate Iltar, the High-Priest; he was their leader; Uranus ordered his arrest."

Caleb asked Kalac "Are you going to Nalta to inform the Archpriest?"

"Yes, I'm going to brief the Archpriest," Kalac said. "I'll tell him that he can send an ambassador to inform Queen Moo that we have taken care of her problem; that Uranus and Chronus have been told about the extortion plot and that the conspirators have been dealt with."

Torr then asked, "What about me?"

"I'll drop you off at the village," Kalac said. "Take a few days off. You need to settle down in your new home. In a few days your new training schedule will be ready. So, let's go, I'll drop you off on my way to Nalta."

Torr was flown back to the village, and Kalac headed for Nalta.

It was about midmorning and Torr figured out that Lena would be at the village clinic; so he headed that way, found her there, and was invited to lunch – at her house.

******

At the Semira Air Base – the hours went by and there was no sign of the general or the others.

It was late in the afternoon – the military control tower informed Uranus that the four vailxi failed to return from their mission.

Esman decided to return to the civilian terminal to inform Iltar. He found Iltar; he was wearing the new outfit; boots, pants, and a jacket.

Iltar had been waiting for a long time, about six hours. The first thing that he asked when he saw Esman was, "What is going on? What happened to the vailxi?"

Esman answered, "They don't know, I found out that the military control tower tried to contact them but there was no response."

"Do you suppose," Iltar asked, "that somehow they found out that they would be arrested when they return?"

"It is possible; but how? Only a few people knew," Esman answered.

"If they knew, it means that they left us holding the bag," Iltar said.

"That's for sure," Esman said; then added, "You must remain in hiding tonight. They don't know about me so in the morning I'll be back at my office and will try to find out if they know what happened and what Uranus is planning on doing about it. Maybe he'll send a vailx to investigate, to see if they did what they were ordered to do."

Iltar said, "Well...there is nothing we can do at this time but to wait and see if they show up tonight or tomorrow morning,"

Then Esman said, "If there is nothing else that we can do I'm going back to Semira. I'll be back tomorrow as soon as I find out what happened and what Uranus is planning on doing. Keep an eye on the military landing pads tonight, just in case they return during the night."

"One last thing," Iltar said. "If I have to escape, the only ship that I could use is Uranus vailx. The military ships, because of their weapons, are guarded by a large number of soldiers. So, try to figure out how I can access Uranus' ship before they close the doors at sunset.

"Do you know how to pilot a vailx?" Esman asked.

"As you know, sometimes I travel with very important kingdom officials including Uranus. A long time ago they gave me flying lessons; it was done so that I could serve as a backup in case something happens to the pilot.

"I was not aware that you knew how to fly a vailx," Esman said; then added, "Well...I'm leaving now, and I'll be back tomorrow as soon I have something to report."

******

The sun was about to hide behind the Western horizon and darkness will soon catch up with the Semira Air Base.

The mechanic that was to sabotage Chronus' vailx entered the parts stock room just before they closed the hangar door; nobody noticed him, he will have all night to sabotage the vailx. The hangar lights can't be turned on so he brought along a small portable light torch.

It wouldn't take long to do what he intended to do, but because the hangar doors can only be opened from the outside he would have to spend the rest of the night waiting for the hangar doors to be opened in the morning.

******

In the morning – the hangar doors were opened from the outside. The mechanic waited a reasonable time and then came out of the stock room with some parts; wrote their assigned part numbers on a board that was nailed to a wall, and then headed for his work area.

******

Not long after the mechanic left, the palace pilot showed up for work and the crew chief told him, "Chronus is back, he arrived yesterday and his landing pad was occupied by the palace vailx. Please park them where they belong."

The pilot said, "I'll be done," and then went and did what the crew chief requested. Now the ships rested on their assigned pads.

******

That same morning – at the palace; the rumor of the day; four vailxi were missing, that they went on a mission and never returned.

Uranus called the usher and told him, "Tell the priest in the communications station to call the base Military Air Operations office and to tell them to send two vailxi to reconnoiter the route that the other four vailxi took on their way to Mohenjo-Daro, and to report their findings to the palace as soon as they return."

******

Two vailxi left the base. Nothing unusual was detected during their flight but when they reached Mohenjo-Daro the pilots were horror-stricken; what used to be a city was now a pile of rubble – in some places skeletons encased in what appeared to be molten glass could be seen.

The two vailxi then raced back to Semira.

******

An hour later they were back. The two pilots reported to the palace what they had seen, and that there were no clues as to what had happened to the four vailxi.

******

About noon time a message from Sais was received at the palace; it seems that the day before, in the late afternoon, the crew of a sailboat on his way to the Delta Ocean Port had witnessed a shower of metallic debris fall from the sky. According to the boat captain the pieces were scattered in four different sites. To Uranus, it implied only one thing; an air battle had taken place, and the vailxi had lost. It meant that the general and the officers were dead.

Upon hearing the news Esman left the palace and headed for the base, he has to tell Iltar.

The first thing that Iltar asked Esman when they met was, "Well...what happened to the vailxi? Do they know?"

Esman answered, "Uranus ordered two vailxi to go all the way to Mohenjo-Daro, you probably saw them this morning when they left the base and when they returned about two hours later."

"Yes I saw them and wondered what was going on." Iltar said; then asked, "Where they able to find the vailxi?"

"No," Esman said. "But Mohenjo-Daro is no more, it was obliterated. What used to be a city is now a pile of rubble, and we have to assume that Harappa was also destroyed."

"But, what happened to the vailxi?" Iltar asked.

"We believe that they were shot down," Esman answered.

"Shot down!!!" Iltar exclaimed; then asked. "How did it happen? In an air battle?"

"Most probable," Esman answered.

"Do they know or suspect who did it?" Iltar asked.

"No, they don't know," Esman said, "but that must be what happened. The crew of a sailboat on his way to the Delta Ocean Port witnessed a shower of metallic debris falling from the sky in four different sites; and that could only happen if they were destroyed in an air battle."

"It looks like if that's what took place." Iltar said.

Esman asked, "So, what are you going to do? Are you still planning on using Uranus vailx to escape?"

"Yes," Iltar said. "But there has been a change of plans. You are staying behind if all the others are dead."

"I'm lucky that the officers are dead," Esman said. "But there is somebody else that knows what you were up to, and if you are planning on returning when Uranus dies or is confined because of his dementia there is something that has to be done as soon as possible – the demise of Amelius before he tells other officials. It has to look as if he lied to Uranus and decided to take his own life."

"I'm counting on you to take care of that," Iltar said. "If everything goes according to plan Chronus will chase me, and that will be his undoing. When Uranus mind worsens or he is about to die you will contact me and I will return. When I return the kingdom officials and the rest of the citizens will be told that I was in a monastery being trained to become a Grand Master."

Esman then said, "I found out that the only ones that are looking for you are the palace guards. It wouldn't be hard for you to steal the palace vailx. Of course, you will have to wear your tunic. Do you still have it?"

"Yes I have it, I saved it, and it's here in the bag with the other four outfits that you bought."

"This is what we'll do," Esman said. "You will need a lot of silver coins, there is still time for me to get them and be back from Semira before the sun goes down.

"When I get back you will go over to the palace hangar and tell the chief that you would like to take the palace vailx out. That you need to go around the field a few times to keep current with your flying skills. They know you, and that you are the pilot back up when travelling with some of the kingdom dignitaries. As soon as I see you take off I'll go over and start asking around if they had seen you, and of course, they will tell me that you are flying Uranus' vailx, circling the base.

"Then, I'll call Chronus and tell him where you are. I'm sure that Chronus will call the crew chief and order him to pick him up at the palace. The chief can fly the vailxi, he has to test fly them after a repair.

"As soon as you see Chronus' vailx land at the palace fly westward, follow the sun so that Chronus can chase you. By the way, where are you planning on going after getting rid of Chronus?"

"I'm heading for Manoa," Iltar answered.

"Manoa!!!...Where is that?" Esman asked.

"It's a port city located on the shores of the south side of the Inland Sea in the Western continent."

"Oh, I see," Esman said. "So, let me go get the silver coins, I'll be back as soon as possible."

******

An hour later Esman returned with the silver coins and found Iltar ready to go – wearing his tunic.

Iltar asked, "Well...anything new?"

Esman answered, "Nobody else knows that they are looking for you, only the palace guards have orders to apprehend you and escort you to the Throne Room to be questioned by Uranus; that means that we can go ahead with our plan to steal the vailx. The mechanics at the hangar are not aware that the palace guards are looking for you. So, let's go, there is still about an hour of daylight."

It didn't take long to go over to where the palace hangar was located. Esman stayed behind, and as expected, the crew chief recognized Iltar, approached him and asked, "What can we do for you today?"

Iltar answered, "As you know I serve as a pilot back up and I haven't flown a vailx for some time now. If you are not working on the palace ship right now I would like to take it out and circle the field a few times, I need to keep current with my flying skills."

"Yes, you can use it, as long as you bring it back before sundown"

"I'll be back on time," Iltar said.

Iltar wasted no time; took the ship out and started circling the base.

Esman then entered the hangar and asked the crew chief, "Have you seen Iltar today?"

"Yes, he took the palace vailx out and is circling the base right now," the chief replied.

"Can I use your communication station?" Esman asked.

"Of course, it's in my office," the chief said.

Esman then went over to the office, and as they had planned on doing called Chronus and told him where he could find Iltar. Then Esman headed for Semira. Their scheme seems to be working.

As expected Chronus called the crew chief and told him, "Bring my ship to the palace, immediately."

"On my way," the crew chief said; then went over to the landing pad, took Chronus' ship out, and headed for the palace.

Once the chief reached the palace Chronus ordered him to return to the base using a chariot and the funicular.

Iltar waited until he saw Chronus' vailx leave the palace, then accelerated and headed westward.

The chase was on, Chronus decided to chase Iltar to his destination, and then to call for some soldiers to be flown in to arrest Iltar and to recover the vailx. Iltar has to land somewhere, he doesn't have that many supplies on board, and so he can't stay airborne indefinitely.

The two vailxi ran at maximum speed heading toward the sun for almost half-an-hour, and then, Iltar vailx exploded; he never knew what hit him, an instant he was there, the next, he was gone.

Chronus had to take evasive action, shredded pieces of Iltar's vailx fluttered in the wind in front of his flight path. Chronus wondered how that could happen, he had never heard of a catastrophic failure like that, then he remembered what Kalac told him; they were planning on killing him in an accident – the saboteur worked on the wrong vailx; for sure it was done the night after his return from Sais when he had to park in Uranus' spot. The saboteur was not aware of the switch and sabotaged the palace vailx instead – next morning the palace pilot moved the ships to their assigned spots; that saved his life.

Chronus then returned to Semira. Darkness prevailed when he reached the base. The crew chief was waiting for him and asked, "Well...were you able to find out where he went?"

"He didn't go anywhere; and like the palace vailx, he was torn to pieces." Chronus answered.

"Do you mean killed?" the chief asked.

"Exactly that," Chronus said. "I was following him, and all of a sudden his vailx disintegrated in front of me. It was me who they were after. I'm sure that whoever was trying to sabotage my ship was not aware that the vailxi were not on their assigned landing pads. I don't know how they were able to do it, but evidently it must have been done at night. So, from now on, every night, post two guards inside the hangar."

Chronus returned to his apartment at the palace.

CHAPTER 29

Next morning – Chronus stopped by Esman office; when Esman saw him enter the office he couldn't believe it, Cronus was supposed to be dead. Fear overwhelmed Esman's being, he thought that somehow they found out about the sabotage and were able to undo whatever the mechanic did to the ship, and that they were on to him.

Esman thought that Chronus came to arrest him but was surprised when Chronus said, "I want to thank you for what you did, for calling me when you saw Iltar at the base."

"It was my duty," Esman said. "I've been looking for Iltar; to report his whereabouts to the palace guards. I was lucky to find him. I called you because he was flying a vailx, and to me it implied that he was planning to steal it to escape. By the way, what happened to him? Were you able to capture him?"

"He is dead," Chronus answered.

"Dead!!! How did it happen?" Esman asked.

"His vailx exploded, right in front of me." Cronus answered.

"Somehow, he was able to sabotage the vailx during the night the day I arrived. Unknown to him the vailxi were not in their assigned pads; the next morning they were repositioned. Evidently, I was the one that was supposed to die, not him.

"Well...anyway, I want to thank you for your initiative and your diligence." Chronus said; then left the room and headed for the Royal Apartments on the fourth floor; he needed to talk to his Father.

Chronus went over to Uranus living quarters and told him, "We have to talk about what is being going on lately."

"Yes...I can imagine," Uranus said.

Chronus then said, "You have to call the other kingdoms and convene a Council of Kings. It is time."

"Time for what?" Uranus asked.

Chronus clarified, "It is time for me to take over as King of Kings."

"What!!! It has never happened; not while the ruling king is still alive, and I'm still alive." Uranus questioned Chronus decision.

"Yes, you are still alive, but your mind is not what it used to be, and look what happened; Iltar was planning on killing me so that eventually he could become the king." Chronus said.

"By the way, have you or the guards been able to find Iltar?" Uranus asked.

"Oh, yes," Chronus said. "And you don't have to worry about him anymore; he is dead."

"Dead!!! How?" Uranus asked.

"Yesterday, just before sundown, Iltar stole the palace vailx. Not long after I started to chase him the palace vailx disintegrated in front of me.

"It is evident that Iltar assumed that I would chase him on my vailx; and he was right about that.

"Somehow, the night of my arrival, Iltar was able to sabotage what he thought was my vailx. He was not aware that the vailxi were not in their assigned landing pads; he sabotaged the palace vailx instead. In the morning the palace pilot returned the vailxi to their assigned pads."

"Well...he died by his own hand," Uranus said; then asked, "And what are you planning on doing with me?"

"The mountain retreat would be your permanent residence, you can have your personal healer, soldiers to serve as guards, and all the servants needed for the upkeep of the place. The palace vailx will be at your disposal whenever you need it."

"Hmm...Well...it doesn't sound that bad," Uranus said. "It is true that my mind is not what it used to be and for that reason I've been delegating some of my authority; and because of that, they used their new found power to extort riches from others. They also tried to kill you with the intention of taking over the throne if there are no heirs when I die. Yes my Son, for the good of the Empire of Atlantis, it is time. I'll convene a Council of Kings. Please take care of informing the other six kings. The meeting to be held in two days."

Chronus then went over to the communications office and sent the invitation to the other six kings.

******

Two days later – six vailxi were seen landing at the palace landing pad, each one unloading a passenger, and then heading for the Semira Air Base.

The meeting, as usual, was held in the Throne Room.

Once everybody was seated the other six kings were informed as to what had happened and what Uranus was planning on doing – abdicate. A long debate ensued; this was something new, it had never happened. At the end it was decided that this time, for the good of the empire, it was the thing to do – to allow Chronus to inherit the throne of Poseidia and to become the King of Kings; the ruler of the Empire of Atlantis.

When Chronus entered the Throne Room that morning he was a prince; when he came out of the room he was a king.

The first thing that Chronus did when he left the room was to contact General Halken who was in charge of all the Poseidia military forces.

Chronus ordered the general to train new officers to lead the Assault Forces, and to arrange for the replacement of the lost vailxi.

Then, following that, Chronus gave orders that all of the heads of the different government institutions report to the palace next day – first thing in the morning.

******

Next morning – in the Throne Room, with the heads of all the kingdom institutions present, including the military, Chronus was introduced by Uranus as the new King of Poseidia and of the Empire of Atlantis.

It was the beginning of a new era for the Empire of Atlantis.

CHAPTER 30

In Muror – the last six days, Torr had been waiting for the call to report for training. The order finally came; his training will start in two days.

*****

Next morning Torr joined the Priest-Scientists on their way to the base, he wanted to see what they had in mind for him the first day of training.

Once Torr reached the base he saw that Kalac was there and he asked himself; what is he doing here so early?

Torr went over to where Kalac was and asked, "How come you are here so early in the morning?"

Kalac replied, "I'm waiting for Ralh to report what's happening in Semira."

"Yes, I was wondering myself what transpired after the four vailxi never returned from Mohenjo-Daro." Torr said.

Kalac then said, "Let's go to Caleb's office and wait there for Ralh to report."

As they headed for the office they went by the white door and Torr stopped and stared at it. Kalac noticed how Torr looked at it and had a big laugh; then asked, "How come you never asked what's on the other side?"

"I thought that if I needed to know I would be told," Torr said.

"Well...I think it's about time that you see what's on the other side," Kalac said; then walking over to the door entered a sequential code on the locking mechanism and the door yielded its well-guarded secret.

Inside; Torr stared in amazement at what he was seeing; in the center of the room there was what appeared to be some kind of a ship, but radically different in shape to the ships he was familiar with. So he asked, "What is that? Can it fly?"

"Yes, it can fly; farther and faster that you can imagine, faster than a light beam can travel in space."

"How can that be?" Torr asked. "The force field in front of the ship can't compress or move out of the way the hydrogen atoms in space; it will require unlimited power."

"It would be impossible to achieve such speeds if we were to use the same technology that we use on the ships that we use in the planet atmosphere." Kalac explained, "Remember during your training, you learned how matter was created; how the hydrogen atom is created.

"Well...that means that if we get rid of the hydrogen or any other atoms in front of the ship there wouldn't be any impediment to content with."

"How is that accomplished?" Torr questioned.

Kalac explained, "By cancelling out the frequencies of creation; the one that creates the ether, the neutron, and the proton; the one that creates the hydrogen atom. Also the frequencies of any small solid particles found in space.

"What we actually do is create a hole of undistorted psychic energy in front of the ship by generating a modulated frequency pulse that cancels out the frequencies of creation.

"As you can see the ship is cone-shaped, like a round pyramid, and the round wide end at the top has a big bulge; that's the pilot cabin, and where all the operational controls are located.

"The bulbous dome that sticks out at the top sends out the frequency pulses to create the void in space."

Torr interrupted and asked, "What type of power plant is used?"

"The ship has an antigravity impulse drive, and it gets an extra help from the cone shape when travelling at high speeds. The tip is at the rear as the ship moves forward through the energy field. As the ship advances the energy field that is left behind is instantly encapsulated by the frequencies of creation that create the hydrogen atoms; those atoms strike the back section of the ship giving it an additional push because of the resultant forces due to the angle of the cone shape.

"The ship is also equipped for dimensional travel; that is, it can translate itself and anything inside, to any place of the universe, at almost the speed of thought."

"How is that possible?" Torr asked.

"You will learn how it is done during your training," Kalac said. "The technology was given to us by the 'Seres'; the race of dimensional travelers that by genetic manipulation of the Homo sapiens created the actual so called human race.

"The technology has to do with the use of a certain frequency that will allow you and the ship to merge, become one, with God's mind; which as you know encompasses the universe. You and the ship will become as big as the universe, and then at the selected arrival point, you and the ship atomic structure can return to God's conceptual size of His universal picture-play."

"Can we take it out?" Torr asked.

"Yes," Kalac replied. "When you finish your training."

"Oh, well," Torr said in a disappointing tone. "I tried anyway," then he asked, "How do you take it in and out of this cave?"

"Because of its size, we can't use the exit-entry tunnel that the other airships use, the only way was to open a hole on the roof of the cave so that it could land and take off vertically," Kalac said. "If you look up you'll notice that the roof of the cave is not natural; it is a metal door; from the outside you can't tell; it looks like the door on the exit-entry tunnel."

******

The ship looked like a cone resting on a horizontal position, supported by three retractable landing gears; a wheel in each one of them. The wide end of the cone had a ring on its circular periphery; segments on this ring when activated help the antigravity impulse engine to perform minute ship positional corrections.

******

After showing Torr the intergalactic ship Kalac said, "Let's go see Caleb and wait for Ralh to report." then, both of them headed for the base commander's office.

The three of them, Caleb, Kalac, and Torr were now in the office waiting for Ralh to report the outcome of the events that had taken place during the last days. While waiting, they exchanged theories; what they thought would be the results.

A knock was heard at the door.

"Come in," Caleb ordered in a loud voice.

It was the priest from the base operations control room, he told Caleb, "Al-El is here and would like to talk to you; he just landed."

"Al-El? Who is that?" Torr asked.

"A member of the 'Seres' race; a race of dimensional travelers that created the present intelligent races; they modified the genetic code of the Homo sapiens that inhabited this planet," Kalac said. "They probably detected what the Atlanteans did at Mohenjo-Daro and Harappa.

"They have a secret outpost located in the Kunlun range of the Uighur Empire. We are the only ones that know about them, and the only ones that they interact with.

"Their purpose; to monitor the progress or evolution of their creation; the human race."

After telling Torr who Al-El was, Caleb looked at the priest and told him, "Let him in as soon as he comes up to your office."

The priest left Caleb's office and soon was back with Al-El; a man much smaller than the average human, with a large pointed head, very large eyes, and a grayish skin. Wearing a uniform that looked like if made from a synthetic gray material with a smooth surface, and had a small round medallion on the center of his chest; this was his language translator.

After the usual greetings, Caleb introduced Torr; the only person in the room that had never met Al-El.

Then Al-El asked, "What is going on? How did it happen? Our sensors detected a huge explosion in the Mohenjo-Daro region; we sent a ship to investigate and the cities of Mohenjo-Daro and Harappa are gone; only rubble is left."

"It was the Atlanteans," Kalac answered. "We uncovered a plot orchestrated by their High-Priest and some rouge generals and officers in charge of their Assault Forces. It seems that they were trying to extort extra compensation from their Military Protection Treaties. Also we suspect that they also intended to kill Chronus so that they could take over the throne when Uranus dies.

"When we found out what they intended to do it was too late, Torr was unable to intercept their vailxi before they destroyed their targets, but he was able to destroy their vailxi when they were returning to Semira. That got rid of the military conspirators. The other conspirator; Iltar; Uranus ordered the palace guards to arrest him."

"I see that you took care of the problem," Al-El said.

"It looks like if we did," Kalac said. "When you came in we were waiting to hear from our man in Poseidia; we'll know if Uranus has everything under control."

"How many ships did you shot down?" Al-El asked Torr.

"Four," Torr answered.

"Hmm...It looks as if you have the makings of a Warrior-Priest. One of these days, if we need help we may have to call on you." Al-El said.

Torr then looking at Al-El said, "If it is possible to translate ourselves across our known universe by breaching our conventional constrains and altering our dimensional conceptions of being – then; if that is true; are there other universes that are beyond our perception because our sensory systems can't perceive their relative mass?"

"Yes, that is true, they exist," Al-El answered; then added, "We can project ourselves there but we prefer to travel and explore our perceived universe."

Al-El had finished saying that when an intermitting beep was heard, it was what they were waiting for; Ralh was calling from Semira. There were only two transmitters-receivers in Muror that were able to communicate with the Semira outpost, one was here in Caleb's office and the other was in the office of the Archpriest, in Nalta.

Caleb flipped a lever and said, "Ralh, go ahead, tell us what you found out."

"Well...it is hard to believe; Chronus has taken over as the King of Kings while Uranus is still alive. There was a meeting of the seven kings and it was decided that because of the recent incident and Uranus mental condition it was the thing to do."

"Well, what do you know," Kalac said. "There is always a first time for everything. Have you heard what is going to happen to Uranus?"

"The rumor is that what was his mountain retreat is going to be his new residence," Ralh said.

"What about Iltar?" Kalac asked.

"He is dead," Ralh said. "He stole the palace vailx to escape, and while Chronus was chasing him the vailx that he stole blew up, it seems that the night before he stole the palace vailx they were not in their assigned landing pads and his intention was to sabotage Chronus' vailx. In the morning the vailxi were repositioned to their assigned landing pads. Later that afternoon unknowingly he stole the vailx that he sabotaged – he died by his own hand."

"And the military? What have you heard?" Kalac asked.

"General Halken – the general of generals – is now in charge of the Assault Forces and is supposed to train and assign new officers. As for the lost vailxi, they are building five new ones."

"Well...that does it, that's all we need to know," Kalac told Ralh. "End of transmission."

Caleb disconnected the receiver.

Al-El then said, "It seems that everything is back to how it should be. There is nothing else to be done here, I'll go back to our outpost and brief our Headmaster as to what took place, and as for Torr, if he can take four days off I would be willing to take him along in our next trip to our planet, that is, if you agree."

"Of course, permission granted," Kalac said.

Al-El then said, "Soon we have to send one of our ships for supplies to our home planet – as you know our planet is in another constellation and as usual we'll be travelling in the dimensional mode. We'll stay there three days and be back on the fourth day."

Torr couldn't believe that this was happening to him, and of course, he accepted.

Al-El then left the room, went back to his ship, left the base, and then headed for the Kunlun outpost.

And as for Torr, he went back to the scribes' workplace, came out of the temple, and looking up to the open sky felt the touch of God's hand upon his soul.

THE END
For now...

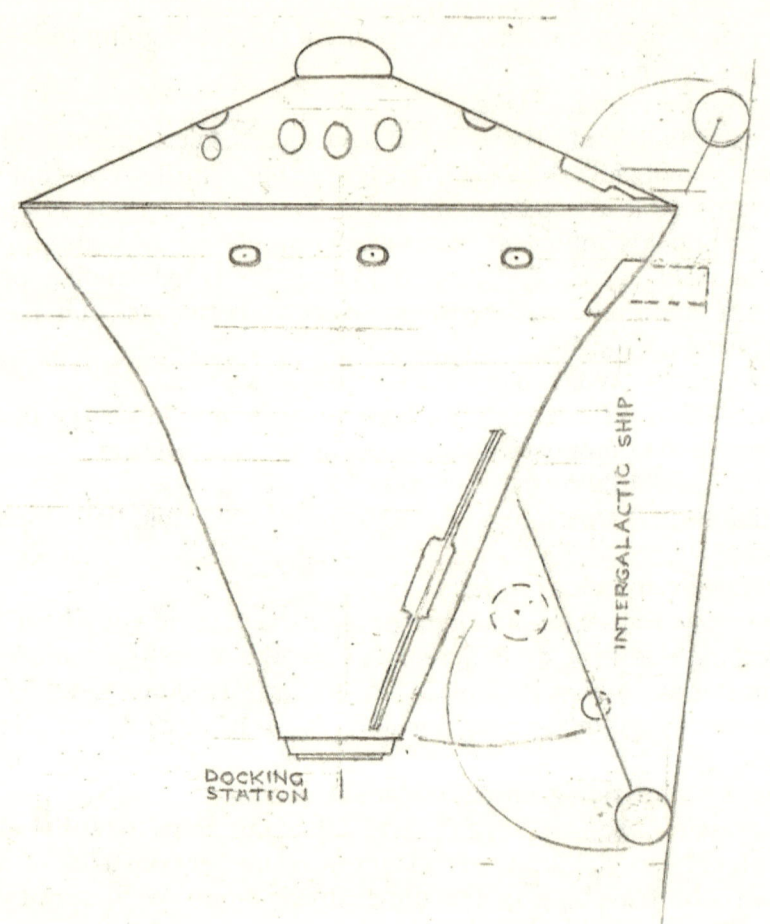

DOCKING
STATION

INTERGALACTIC SHIP